Sword Art Online Alternative
Gun Gale Online
II
2nd Squad Ja[...]

Keiichi Sigsawa

ILLUSTRATION BY
Kouhaku Kuroboshi

SUPERVISED BY
Reki Kawahara

Sword Ar[...] [...]ernative
GU[...][...]E
ON[...]

2nd Squad [...]am: Start:

CONTENTS

DESIGN: BEE-PEE

GUN GALE ONLINE
2nd Squad Jam: Start.

Sword Art Online Alternative

GUN GALE ONLINE II

2nd Squad Jam: Start:

Keiichi Sigsawa

ILLUSTRATION BY
Kouhaku Kuroboshi

SUPERVISED BY
Reki Kawahara

NEW YORK

SWORD ART ONLINE Alternative Gun Gale Online, Vol. 2
KEIICHI SIGSAWA

Translation by Stephen Paul
Cover art by Kouhaku Kuroboshi

SWORD ART ONLINE Alternative Gun Gale Online Vol. II
©KEIICHI SIGSAWA 2015
First published in Japan in 2015 by KADOKAWA CORPORATION, Tokyo.
English translation rights arranged with KADOKAWA CORPORATION, Tokyo,
through TUTTLE-MORI AGENCY, INC., Tokyo.

English translation © 2018 by Yen Press, LLC

Yen On
1290 Avenue of the Americas
New York, NY 10104

Visit us at yenpress.com
facebook.com/yenpress
twitter.com/yenpress
yenpress.tumblr.com
instagram.com/yenpress

First Yen On Edition: September 2018

Yen On is an imprint of Yen Press, LLC.
The Yen On name and logo are trademarks of Yen Press, LLC.

Library of Congress Cataloging-in-Publication Data
Names: Sigsawa, Keiichi, 1972– author. | Kuroboshi, Kouhaku, illustrator. |
    Kawahara, Reki, supervisor. | Paul, Stephen (Translator), translator.
Title: Second Squad Jam : start / Keiichi Sigsawa ; illustration by Kouhaku Kuroboshi ;
    supervised by Reki Kawahara ; translation by Stephen Paul.
Description: First Yen On edition. | New York, NY : Yen On, September 2018. |
    Series: Sword art online alternative gun gale online ; Volume 2
Identifiers: LCCN 2018028790 | ISBN 9781975353841 (pbk.)
Subjects: | CYAC: Fantasy games—Fiction. | Virtual reality—Fiction. | Role
    playing—Fiction.
Classification: LCC PZ7.1.S537 Se 2018 | DDC [Fic]—dc23
LC record available at https://lccn.loc.gov/2018028790

ISBNs: 978-1-9753-5384-1 (paperback)
       978-1-9753-5390-2 (ebook)

10 9 8 7 6 5 4 3 2 1

LSC-C

Printed in the United States of America

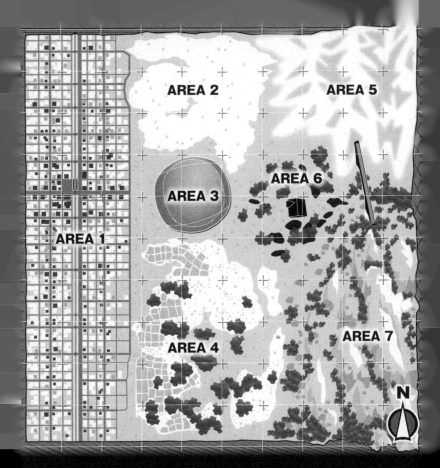

AREA 1 : Town

AREA 2 : Hills

AREA 3 : Dome

AREA 4 : Fields / Woods

AREA 5 : Snowy Mountains

AREA 6 : Plains

AREA 7 : Rocky Mountains

PROLOGUE

PROLOGUE

"Uh, what? Um... Well...well, er, this is...um..."

Karen Kohiruimaki was terribly confused.

How did she get herself into this situation?

She didn't know. She just didn't know.

Her entire six-foot-tall frame, a considerable height for a nineteen-year-old Japanese woman, was pressed flat against the wallpaper. She felt the cold of the hard surface through her clothes.

Immediately next to her head, which was covered in short black hair, was a right arm.

It belonged to a man, easily identified by the thick muscle, and he was pressing against the wall near her left ear.

Naturally, he stood right before her eyes. Both his burly chest, which stretched the fabric of his T-shirt, and his piercing gaze were extremely close.

Oh...this must be...that famous...wall-slamming mating ritual...

It was really the only thing Karen's mind was composed enough to process.

Wall slam.

The recently popularized term referred to the act of a man pressing a girl's back to the wall and forcefully placing his hand against the wall over her shoulder.

As for what the man expected to get from this forward behavior, assuming he wasn't desperate for money, it was usually to gain her attention and favor for romance. In other words, a forceful step taken by a man running out of patience for a wishy-washy, noncommittal girl.

She understood the concept, but she'd never expected it would happen to her. This was the kind of thing that happened to the protagonists of romance manga for girls, not to Karen.

Well, it's a good thing that he's at least kind of tall, she thought ruefully.

He was shorter than she was but still a good five foot nine or so. At the very least, it looked like a proper wall slam this way.

He was a handsome guy who seemed at least a few years older than she was. In a rich baritone voice, he shouted, "Have you ever truly, passionately loved someone in your life? Have you ever been in love with someone you'd sacrifice your entire life for?"

She was so flustered that she couldn't have lied on the spot. Instead, as if she'd been given a truth serum, Karen answered, "I—I haven't…"

In a tapestry of emotions ranging from sadness to anguish to fury, the man yelled, "Then you have no idea how I feel right now!"

Huh…? Why did this…? How did this…?

Question marks popped into Karen's head, and rather than resolving, they just sat there, piling up inside.

That happened at 3:42 PM on Sunday, March 16th, 2026.

Nineteen days before the second Squad Jam.

CHAPTER 1

The Soldiers' Tea Party

SECT.1

CHAPTER 1
The Soldiers' Tea Party

Sunday, February 15th, 2026—about one thirty in the afternoon...

On this cloudy, gloomy day in Tokyo, one apartment in a high-rise building was full of bright, raucous cheers.

"Ooh, wow!"

"Yes, yes, yes!"

"That was a really good one!"

"Just brilliant."

"This is incredible!"

"She's so fast!"

They sat in a relaxed, cozy living room with white walls. Atop a cream-white rug were six teenage girls in high school uniforms, excitedly watching a video on the forty-two-inch flat-screen TV in the corner of the room.

Five of the six were black-haired Japanese girls. The last girl had blond hair and white skin.

Behind them was a slightly older and much taller Japanese woman. She sat down, tucking her legs sideways, and said, "It feels weird having people cheering for me," as she watched the girls' heads bob.

Then she added, "Especially when the part coming up is where we were shooting at each other..."

The imagery on the large LCD screen was made of computer graphics—so realistic that it might as well have been real life.

Despite the sun being high overhead, the sky was as red as late sunset—the camera taking an aerial view of a spaceship out of some sci-fi movie sticking out of a swamp.

"I wanna see that battle again! Can we rewind it a bit, Karen?" asked one of the teenage girls, her braids swinging as she turned to look over her shoulder.

"Go ahead," Karen Kohiruimaki, the towering resident of the apartment, said with a smile. "As many times as you want."

Now that she had permission, the girl hammered the button on the nearby remote that rewound a certain number of seconds. The frame changed with each press of the button until she got to the point she wanted.

The CG footage showed a wide-open intersection in what looked like an upscale foreign suburb. The intersection was full of scattered garbage, like abandoned tires, shopping carts, and suitcases, and its asphalt was dry and cracked. The camera was filming at a diagonal angle from a medium height.

Four men wearing camouflage fatigues appeared on the scene, holding black rifles. These, too, were CG characters.

The men proceeded into the intersection, scanning the area very carefully. They all wore masks that covered their faces. No voices were audible, either.

"Here she comes…," muttered one of the girls, right as a suitcase in the frame split open. At first, it looked like it had popped open on its own, like a grilled clam.

"There she is!"

But inside was a girl in pink.

She was small, not even five feet tall. Everything about her, from her combat fatigues to her boots to her gloves to her hat to her clip pouches, even the strange-looking device in her hands, was pink.

The device spit flames, emitting a high-pitched automatic-gunfire rattle through the TV speakers; it was a gun.

The man closest to the girl in pink took bullets to the face and body, the bullet wounds glowing red and spraying fine red particles. It wasn't actual, gory blood but simple CG bullet-hit effects made of nothing but colored light.

He toppled over on the spot, and a red marker reading DEAD appeared over his head. He was gone.

The pink girl continued shooting at the next-closest man. He fired back with his rifle, but the girl was so incredibly fast that not a single shot hit her. He, on the other hand, became riddled with bullets.

With her second opponent killed in as many seconds, the girl in pink leaped and took cover behind the dead body. The remaining two men pointed their rifles at her, but one hesitated to fire. The other one tried anyway and failed to hit the tiny target, who used the body as a shield. She killed him instead.

She rolled around on the ground like a top until the final man erupted in a torrent of bullet-wound effects.

Within seconds, the girl had slaughtered all four of her opponents and moved on with tremendous speed. She was out of frame so fast, it was practically a joke.

The teenage girl hit the pause button on the remote, looked back over her shoulder again, and exclaimed, "Every time I see it, I'm still impressed, Karen!"

Karen smiled uncomfortably. "I could only pull that off as Llenn."

The smaller girl had a powerful voice for such a tiny body. "You two are the same! The player's the one who's moving the avatar! So it's not Llenn, champion of Squad Jam, and then Karen—you're both the same person!"

In the year 2026, video games were undergoing a tremendous leap forward.

It was the age of full-dive virtual reality games, where the game shut off all bodily sensations and transmitted its own sensory information to the brain, making it seem like you'd actually been transported to a completely different place.

In other words, as long as you had a computer, the game software, and large goggle-shaped headwear called an AmuSphere, you could travel to another world from the safety of your room.

The AmuSphere interrupted bodily signals and sent false sensory information directly to the brain. It effectively put the player into a waking dream of sorts, in which they controlled a VR avatar as if its body were the player's own.

It was truly the game of dreams: actually playing as another person.

There was an abundance of full-dive VR games in all styles you could possibly imagine. One particular example was a VRMMORPG (virtual reality massively multiplayer online role-playing game) with gun battles.

This game was *Gun Gale Online*, or *GGO*.

It was set on a ruined, postapocalyptic Earth where humanity had returned on spaceships and now ran around with guns. Sometimes you battled monsters, sometimes other player characters.

And you fought with guns.

There were sci-fi optical-beam guns as well as live-ammo guns based on real-world models. This was a game for gun fanatics—a place where you could get whatever gun you wanted and engage in shoot-outs in a safe, virtual setting.

On top of that, *GGO* did not officially outlaw the exchange of in-game currency for real electronic cash. So it developed a whole economy of professional players who literally played like their livelihoods depended on it—that was how they made their money.

In *GGO*, there was a battle-royale tournament to determine who the strongest player was. It was called the Bullet of Bullets, or the BoB.

The BoB was the biggest thing in *GGO*. There had been three tournaments already, and each one was bigger than the previous.

Then somebody got the idea, "What if instead of players fighting for themselves, there was a team-based battle-royale event instead?" So he petitioned Zaskar, the American company that ran *GGO*. By signing on as a financial sponsor, he convinced them to hold an in-game event based on his idea.

It would be a battle royale, like the BoB, but with teams of up to six players each. They called it Squad Jam, or SJ for short. In other words, a place for you and your squad to get in there and mix it up.

Squad Jam had started as an individually funded mini-competition, and event organizers had run it just two weeks earlier, on February 1st. It was nothing like the BoB, which was big enough to have a livestream on the major Internet channels, but SJ was pretty exciting nonetheless.

The only way to watch the progress of the battle was at the bar that served as the event base, on the live feed there. In a special map exactly ten kilometers large, twenty-three teams engaged in a furious firefight for supremacy.

The crowd downed their drinks at the bar as they watched the event unfold. After one hour, twenty-eight minutes, and 49,810 shots fired, the winner was a surprising two-person team, the minimum allowed size.

One of the two was a burly man with excellent firing accuracy by the handle of M.

And the other member...was Llenn.

Karen Kohiruimaki's little-girl avatar, dressed all in pink.

On the screen, a truck was rolling down a suburban street.

It was a simple military-style truck, with armored plates patched along the driver's side and roof. It raced down the cracked asphalt, flattening littered junk with huge tires, until it came to a stop before a mansion.

"So that truck was how you guys got there so fast from the edge of the map, Saki?" Karen asked the girl with braids.

"Right!" she replied, whipping her head around. Her name was Saki Nitobe. She was a second-year student at the high school attached to Karen's prestigious women's university, and she was also the captain of the gymnastics team.

On the screen, a large, heavyset woman exited the front passenger seat of the truck. She was over six feet tall, quite muscular and with a broad chest, like a professional wrestler. Without the braids on either side of her head, she would not have appeared particularly feminine. She seemed to be well past her mid-thirties.

She wore a camouflage uniform with fine green spots all over it. There was a large backpack in her hand.

This powerful-looking soldier, going by the name of Eva, was Saki's avatar in *GGO*.

"Mmm. You just seem so sca— I mean, tough...," Karen said, trying to hide her initial reaction, but Saki caught it instantly.

She puffed out her little cheeks. "Hey! Karen, you were going to call me scary!"

"Sorry, sorry. But...you kind of are," Karen admitted with a smile.

One of the other girls, who wore her hair short, smiled innocently. "Yeah, Boss is the meanest looking of all of us!"

Her name was Kana Fujisawa. She had hair down to her shoulders and wore a bold, confident look. Kana was another second-year student like Saki, and the two were old friends. She was the vice-captain of the gymnastics team.

So Saki is known as "Boss" in both real life and virtual reality, Karen realized.

Saki pointed at the screen. "Same to you, Kanacchi! Look at her avatar, Karen! Look how buff Sophie is!"

Another character was descending from the bay of the truck. She was shorter but even wider, with a menacing face. This was Sophie.

Everything about her squatness and solidity brought the image of a fantasy-based dwarf to mind. Her long brown hair was pulled into a single rough ponytail behind her head. Sophie also carried a heavy-looking Russian PKM machine gun. It was a vicious weapon capable of producing a hail of bullets.

"Ha-ha-ha. You both look very tough." Karen chuckled, remembering the moment when she'd decided to shoot her opponents dead.

She'd imagined that this group of girls was insulting her behind her back, and she'd sought out her model gun in a rage. Ultimately, that had ended up leading her to enter Squad Jam—quite a bit of foreshadowing.

You never know where life will send you next, Karen thought wistfully.

"Ooh! Next is me!" another girl exclaimed, raising her pale hand.

This was the white girl with blue eyes and golden-blond hair that ran in clean waves down to her shoulders. She was the same height as the other girls, making her quite short for a foreigner. Her Japanese was extremely good; there was nothing off about her pronunciation.

"Okay, Milana," Karen replied.

Milana Sidorova was a first-year high school student. Her parents worked for a Russian trading business. Milana had therefore bounced between Tokyo and Moscow since childhood, and she'd been attending this school since the second year of junior high.

On the screen, another character, with a long, narrow gun, stepped out of the driver's seat. This was Milana's avatar, Tohma. She was about five foot nine with a slender build and wore a green knit cap over her glossy, short black hair. Like the rest of them, she was dressed in camo. Her weapon was the famous Russian semi-auto sniping rifle the Dragunov.

Saki paused the footage. "Can you believe it? Mi knows how to drive a stick shift! Her father loves cars, so he taught her himself in Russia."

"Ohhh, so that's how...," Karen murmured. Anything you could do in real life, you could do in *GGO*.

"Moving on!" Saki said, resuming the video. The next character leaped out of the truck bay.

This woman looked to be much older than the others, with

short red hair and freckles. She was tall and had broad shoulders, like a hearty, tough mother. She, too, had a PKM machine gun. On her back was a pack holding spare barrels and ammunition boxes. There were three plasma grenades hanging from either side of the pack.

"Ooh, yes! That's me!" shouted a girl from the side of the snack-laden table. She was quite unlike the woman on the screen—more of a classic pretty Japanese girl with a bob cut, like a traditional doll.

Her real-world name was Shiori Noguchi, and she was a second-year high school student. In *GGO*, her name was Rosa.

Karen stared at Rosa's intimidating face—one she had stared down during Squad Jam—and then looked back at the adorable girl who'd been controlling her.

"So that was you, Shiori...," she said, letting the realization sink in.

"Heh-heh-heh!" Shiori laughed to cover her embarrassment. Karen beamed back.

On the screen, a fifth team member got down from the truck. This one had long, flowing blond hair under a green cap and looked like she was in her early twenties, younger than the rest. She had sunglasses and beautiful features, like some glamorous actress. Slung over her back was a Dragunov sniper rifle.

"Um, that one is...me...," said the girl with the longest hair of the group, timidly raising her hand. She was a first-year student by the name of Moe Annaka. Since her character's name was Anna, that made her the group member with the closest in-game and real-name resemblance.

When Karen didn't comment, Moe shrank even smaller than before and said, "I...I'm sorry...for having such a big-shot avatar."

"Pardon?" Karen asked, honestly befuddled.

Saki, the boss, interrupted to say, "Moe feels a bit out of place for having an avatar that looks like a super-cool Hollywood actress. We keep saying she doesn't need to be bashful!"

"Oh, I see..."

On the screen, the last of the team descended. She was the shortest of the group, though still at least five foot three. Her hair was silver and very short. The sharp, cunning look in her eyes was reminiscent of a fox. Her gear and camo were just like the others', but she had a pistol holster on her waist, like Boss's. In her hands was a Russian submachine gun, the PP-19 Bizon.

"Ooh, ooh! That's me! I'm the one playing Tanya!" said a rather tomboyish girl, raising her hand. She had very short hair and almost looked like a very pretty boy wearing feminine clothing. But of course, she was a girl and a first-year member of the gymnastics team—Risa Kusunoki.

"Risa's the one who looks the most like her avatar!" boasted Saki. True, their hair was identical in length, just different colors. Tanya, the avatar, looked a little meaner, though.

"And there you go! That's your introduction to the *GGO* characters for the entire high school gymnastics team!" Saki finished.

Karen thanked her. "Um...are you sure you want to watch the rest?" she continued, a bit hesitant.

"Of course we will why wouldn't we that's the whole point it's why we came we're watching this!"

The responses were just as rapid-fire as their guns. Saki had to hold up a hand to silence the others.

"Of course we'll watch it! We want a full explanation of just how you killed us, Karen! Then we'll learn from our mistakes, study up, and win it all in the next SJ!"

✳   ✳   ✳

In the Squad Jam two weeks ago, Karen's—make that Llenn's—last and toughest foe was none other than these girls.

Two days after the event, by sheer coincidence, their real-life identities had been exposed to one another, and since then, Karen and the six gymnastics team members from the academy's high school had traded greetings when they passed one another.

Then it turned into short conversations, then longer ones, then chat sessions, and finally, since they didn't always have time on the spot, Karen finally tossed out an idea: "Why don't you come hang out at my apartment sometime when you don't have school? It's just one station away if you take the subway, and not even that long if you walk…"

As soon as she said that, she was stunned at herself. *Look how forward you've become at inviting others to socialize!*

And at the same time, she thought, *Maybe I got overconfident and said something really inappropriate.* She felt embarrassed.

If someone older than them, whom they hadn't known for very long, invited them over to her place, would they get defensive? And was she pressuring them not to decline the offer? Should they start off by hanging out at a coffee shop first?

It felt like she'd been strangely proactive since Squad Jam. Was she actually heading in the wrong direction with this new personality development?

But their response was an avalanche.

"What can we really we're going oh for sure I'd love to I'll go yes please let us come over!"

All six of them leaped at the offer at once, and for the first time since she'd come to Tokyo, Karen had friends(?) over at her place.

Although they didn't have school that day, the girls still had practice, so they were wearing their uniforms. Karen served them a feast of junk food and tea. Once the six had eaten their fill, Saki asked whether she could turn on the television.

When Karen gave her permission, she used the TV's Internet connection to display a video of their battle.

It was a recut, hour-long edit of the SJ combat that the developers had put together to show off all the best bits of competition. You could see this footage from within *GGO*, while on a full dive, or you could use your online connection to view it as a video in the real world.

Karen was quite surprised by this decision, but once she'd given permission, she couldn't just take it away. It had been two weeks since the SJ event, and she hadn't watched any of the footage yet.

In fact, she hadn't played *GGO* since then.

This was for a combination of reasons. After all the damage she'd done in Squad Jam, she felt very satisfied and fulfilled with the experience. Plus, there was the matter of what had happened with M during the event, which made her a bit afraid to go back.

"This is the perfect opportunity! Let's watch it for research!" Saki said, the younger girl seizing the reins. And so, they watched the digest video.

"You're all so dedicated…," Karen mused, not unlike a grandmother. The girls were watching their battle over and over, reflecting on their mistakes and trying to learn from them.

"Well, of course we are! It's part of our team activities!"

"It's what?"

What did *GGO* have to do with gymnastics? Karen found that quite confusing.

"Oh, that's right. I haven't told you that yet." Saki paused the video and, as team leader, spoke for the rest of the group. "Last April, just after we got three new first-year members, our teamwork was in a terrible state."

"Oh…really?" Karen asked, surprised. They looked so happy together now. "I would never have imagined it…"

"Yes, it was terrible. It's not like we'd start punching each other in the face when we met, but when we did routines together, we were completely off—no rhythm… So on the college coach's recommendation, we tried training with full-dive VR. Karen, do you know what a full-dive sports simulator is?"

"No," she said, although she could guess by the name.

"It's where you use the AmuSphere and an avatar with your same height to practice," Saki explained. "It's a way to reduce the danger of attempting dangerous techniques the first time, so the more flexible coaches are experimenting with it now."

"Ohhh…"

Karen was impressed. She'd used VR only for fun (that is, for *GGO*), so she hadn't realized it could also be practical and useful.

"In the end, it always comes down to real physical strength, and it's only a simulation, but it helps you practice the movements. If there were in-dive tournaments, that would be a different story, but that's not a thing yet. I hear they might start trying that sometime, though."

"That's helpful. So the reason you all moved so smoothly was that you had a lot of practice in there."

"Heh-heh-heh. But actually, we were so out of sync and such bad teammates that our coach threw in the towel on the simulator practice!" Saki said.

Behind her, Kana picked up a marshmallow off the table and rudely threw it to mimic their coach. "Catch!"

"Got it!" On the other side was Risa, the tomboy, who barely had to move her head as she caught the arcing marshmallow in her mouth.

Nice one! Karen silently cheered.

Their gymnastics pedigree was legitimate. The aim of the marshmallow tosser and the receiver were perfect. And it seemed like they could do that over and over without a mistake. From an even longer distance, too.

That would explain how they'd been able to execute a superhuman maneuver like catching a thrown clip directly in a gun to reload it.

"Now, now! This is another person's house!" Saki scolded in a rather old-fashioned way. She continued, "Our coach told us, 'First you need to be a *team*. We can talk after that.' So we tried to figure out what to do. And our answer was..."

"I get it. You tried out the game."

"Exactly! Party play in a VR game will naturally involve us all in the pursuit of a common goal! And we also hoped that by using avatars rather than ourselves, it might help us get over our real-world issues with each other."

"Ooh...," Karen murmured, both surprised and impressed.

Real-world issues were exactly what Karen was dealing with. She hadn't been able to look at her tall, gangly self, so she'd fled to the virtual realm for a solution.

"At first, we were playing a different VR game. It was one where everyone goes on an adventure on a desert island. But we got bored of that in a week, well before we started getting along. It seemed like games weren't going to help us, either, so we decided to take a gamble on *GGO*, because what could be more different from what we do in real life than a game about killing people with guns?"

"I see. And once you tried it…"

"It worked out great! I mean, using guns to shoot monsters and have gunfights is just so unreal that you don't even register what you're doing, right? But suddenly, we were all hooked. We created a squadron named Gymnastics Club, and now we play it whenever we have the time."

A *squadron* was the name for a player team in *GGO*—when you and your friends formed a group. In fantasy-themed games, it'd be called a guild.

"We did squabble along the way, but at the end of it all, this is the result. We fought so many monsters and other players and saved each other in so many deadly battles that we're all best friends now!"

"That's wonderful!" Karen exclaimed, beaming.

They'd started the game to work on their team cohesion, and it had taken them all the way to being runners-up in SJ, so they'd also proved they had a talent for it. Of course, *she* was the winner, but that was due to M's help, with a good amount of luck mixed in.

"And that's why we're studying hard to try to win the second Squad Jam, if it ever happens!"

"Huh? So…it's not for your team?"

"Well, that too! So when we watch our battle scene up ahead, we need your help, Karen—I mean, Llenn the Pink Maiden of

Manslaughter! Give us your most merciless advice as to why we lost!"

The other five echoed her request.

"Uh, if you insist…" Karen smiled weakly.

For about an hour after that, Karen watched the battle between herself and the six high schoolers unfold. They rewound again and again, sometimes changing the camera-angle option, so that she could answer their questions.

At the lake where they first fought: "When Tohma sniped me, I thought I was a goner. That was an incredible shot. If it was just a bit higher, it would've been an insta-kill. M's quick reaction saved my life."

After they disembarked in the desert: "Huh? This part where we split up…? Hmm, I'm not sure how to explain it… It was his business, so I can't be very explicit about it, but we fought over a misunderstanding. He didn't want to keep doing the event, so he wanted to kill me and become the team leader so he could resign for us. But we cleared that up later. And he fought at the end, remember? It wasn't some plan to use the team leader as bait—but the strange thing is, that was kind of how it turned out…"

Their first engagement in the desert: "I think the reason I was able to beat Tanya was because I was smaller. It was a really tough fight. I heard the bullets flying right behind me."

When Boss shot her: "Boss's silencer gun surprised me! That's a scary weapon. I never noticed it, and I walked right into your trap. You caught me being way too careless. If it hadn't hit my magazine, I would've died here."

When she ran away from the hail of machine-gun fire: "I had no idea you could use plasma grenades as a shield. It was just a wild attempt to do something, because it was the only tool I had left…"

When she started fighting back and beat Anna: "I thought I was dead again when Rosa had her machine gun pointed at me. How many times had it been that day...? Oh, and M's sniping here doesn't have a bullet line. He aims and shoots all on his own. It's not fair, but you can't do anything about it."

After her incredible one-on-one with Boss started: "When you shot my chest, the scanner saved me...which was a total coincidence. I doubt that's going to work again. Otherwise, everyone would be trying it."

At the final confrontation: "Oh, uh, P-chan is the name of my P90. And don't worry about that! I used it as a shield! That's on me! And I can just buy another one! I'll dye it pink again!"

When the viewing party and study session for the girls was over, Karen asked, "I still have more snacks. Anyone want some?"

"Of course!" cheered all six girls in perfect unison. There was no overlap. Indeed, they were a very close-knit group now.

Karen offered them the rest of the pile of snacks she'd bought for the occasion. If it turned out to be overkill, she would either give the leftovers to her niece or eat them herself, but it seemed like that wasn't going to be necessary.

They certainly ate a lot for being so small. And none of them was overweight. That was the power of the athlete's lifestyle.

Bag of savory consommé-flavor potato chips in hand, Saki said, "Karen, I'm just going to ask you straight out. If there's a second Squad Jam, will you enter?"

"Hmm..."

Karen stopped eating her salted-kelp-flavor chips, a personal favorite that she bought in large quantity although it wasn't very popular with the other girls, and thought this over.

She'd struck gold and won the first Squad Jam. Given where she'd been before that, it was far more than she could have expected. She was utterly fulfilled by the result.

But at the same time, there was much left to do. Her own carelessness had nearly gotten her killed several times. She'd lost her beloved P90.

There was a part of her that smoldered with the thought that, if given another chance, she could do it better this time. There weren't any other big team-based tournaments, and while the experience was scary, the thrills of battle and the fun of doing well were undeniable.

If Pitohui invited her and she was teamed up with M again, maybe she would consider it, she had thought at times. But reflecting on M's abnormal behavior toward the end of the last one, and whatever it was about Pitohui's real life that had prompted it, she couldn't simply sign up without any reservations.

In fact, it was more likely that she would turn down the offer if she got it now—although she wasn't planning to just quit *GGO* forever.

Speaking of Pitohui—the day after Squad Jam, she sent a brief message saying "You did it, congrats!" but had maintained radio silence since then. Perhaps she was busy at work?

M hadn't really contacted her, either, and it wasn't like she had much to say to him. So that's where things sat.

"A second one... Unless something big comes up, I think it's pretty unlikely I'd play... I do have areas for improvement, but I can't deny I feel like I got everything I wanted out of it. Plus, I was only teammates with M for the day, pretty much," Karen admitted honestly.

"Oh, I see... I guess I'm both happy and disappointed. I'm happy I won't have to face off against a powerful rival, but I'm disappointed that I won't get the chance to make up for last time!" Saki said, speaking for the rest of the group.

Karen sensed the fighting spirit in the other girls' stares. It seemed to her that they were more motivated now, and she would certainly lose if they fought again...but she spoke not a word of it.

Instead, she said, "But if there *is* a second one, would it really happen that soon?"

"Well, I don't know. But if someone puts up the money for it like the first time, I imagine it would be pretty easy to get set up."

"I see. So it depends on the sponsor."

*   *   *

That was all for the topic of Squad Jam. They continued chatting nonstop until five o'clock in the evening. The topics ranged from real life to *GGO* and back to real life again. The gymnastics-team girls talked about themselves a lot, but they asked Karen plenty of questions, too. And Karen found it surprisingly easy to discuss her complex about her height and how she got started playing *GGO*.

She even told them about how she'd cut her hair short without explaining why to anyone, causing her elder sister's family living on the floor above to interrogate her about a possible romantic breakup.

Karen never thought she'd speak about the height complex she'd struggled with for over a decade to anyone other than her closest friends. But here she was, spilling all her secrets to a group of younger girls she'd only just met. She had to marvel at the effect that *GGO* and Squad Jam had brought to her life.

Sometime in the past, Karen had heard the saying, "The more you worry about your troubles, the more they hurt you. Just blow them away. Toss them out like last week's garbage. If you get rid of them, you even save yourself the trouble of having to worry about getting rid of them." Now she was marveling at just how true that was.

"Um, is that a P90? May I take a look at it?"

"I wanna see, too!"

"Me too!"

The group of six gathered around the P90 air gun hanging from her clothes rack.

"I've never touched a model gun in real life!"

They all marveled.

That made sense, when Karen thought about it. Teenage girls didn't usually buy gun models. They were toys for a target audience of eighteen years and older. And even college students like her didn't buy them.

The topic turned to real-life hobbies, so Karen asked the girls about her favorite singer-songwriter at the moment, Elza Kanzaki. It was little surprise, given her exploding popularity, that all of them had heard of her. They didn't have her entire discography, however, so Karen decided to put on one of her albums for background music.

"I wish I could see her perform live, but the tickets are hard to come by. I keep trying to order them, but it never works out," Karen grumbled.

"Well, at least you'd be able to afford them if they were actually on sale!" Saki pointed out. "Concert tickets are too expensive these days! We can't buy them, because we have other stuff to use our allowance on! And *GGO*'s monthly fee isn't cheap, either!"

The rest of the girls nodded at this. True, three thousand yen every month was a lot for a high school girl to spend only on *GGO*. It was a reminder to Karen that her family was quite well-off in the grand scheme of things.

Then the topic changed again.

"Karen, are you on spring break already? It must be nice to be in college."

The high schoolers still had over a month of classes left until their break in late March. Either way, they'd be attending the same college as her in two or three years. Then they'd be her underclassmen.

"I'm on vacation already. I'm planning to go back home to Hokkaido this week."

"I'm so jealous! You get to dive all you want!" said Shiori, the traditional beauty with the bob cut.

Karen shook her head. "I'm going back to my parents', so I won't be gaming at all. I'm not taking my AmuSphere with me."

"Oh, you aren't?"

"It'll be a pain if my parents catch me playing. They probably know about the *SAO* Incident, anyway. So no *GGO* for a while."

"Watch out—we're going to get a lot better by the time you come back," Shiori cautioned, fixing Karen with a look.

But they're already plenty tough, Karen thought as she envisioned Shiori's avatar, the machine gunner Rosa.

"Good luck. I bet you guys can totally win the next Squad Jam!" she said, giving them a huge smile.

Saki couldn't help being honest, though.

"Hrmm... I wish you would compete with us..."

CHAPTER 2

SECT.2

Second Squad Jam

CHAPTER 2
Second Squad Jam

On February 17th, two days after her hangout with Saki and her friends, Karen returned home to Hokkaido.

A cold front had descended, so it was a brutal negative four degrees Fahrenheit, but inside the house, it was much warmer than her apartment in Tokyo.

Karen's parents were taken aback by her short hair. Apparently, her sister hadn't said a word about it. They demanded to know the reason why, but she wasn't going to tell them, "In a virtual murder simulator, I shot a bunch of people to death and killed the last one with a knife blade across the neck, and...it felt so good, I needed a haircut." No way could she say that.

It wasn't because of a broken heart, either. Like with her sister, it was very difficult to figure out a vague enough explanation that would satisfy them.

As she'd told Saki, she hadn't taken the AmuSphere back with her, so there was no *GGO* time. She did have the laptop with the game loaded onto it, so she could check her messages, but nothing had come in from Pitohui or M. She was curious about them but not to the point that she'd reach out to bug them.

There was one very excitable message from Eva, aka Boss—Saki's character—that read *Finals are killing me! I wanna hang out and be lazy at your place again, Karen! I wanna eat snacks! I wanna play GGO! I wanna shoot guns!*

It seemed very in character for her to send a message specifically in *GGO*, even though Karen had shared her smartphone information with her.

*   *   *

One week later, it was Tuesday, February 24th.

"Yoo-hoo! Welcome to Hokkaido, Kohi! Must be cold for a Tokyo person, huh? Ain't it?"

Karen's high school friend Miyu Shinohara came back from her overseas vacation during spring break and visited the house to hang out. She was the one who'd taught Karen all about the ways of VR gaming last summer. If not for Miyu, the Karen of today would not exist, and certainly neither would Llenn.

"Mmm! That short hair suits you! Can I take a picture? Can I? Now turn around! Now face forward again! Yes, very nice! Now let's take off some of those clothes, shall we?"

Miyu hadn't seen Karen's short hair in person yet, and she was very excited about it, snapping photos endlessly with her smartphone.

Karen, who hadn't removed a single article of clothing, said, "You've changed plenty yourself, Miyu. It looks good."

"Right? Well, I can make anything look good," Miyu replied. She often changed her hairstyle on a whim—today's look was wavy semi-long brown hair, with red-framed glasses instead of her usual contacts.

Miyu was shorter than Karen, but at five foot five, she was still on the tall side for a Japanese woman. She'd played tennis in both middle and high school, so her affinity for physical exercise was considerably high.

She went to a local college in Hokkaido and was also a heavy VR gamer. As long as she could get online, she played every single day. Her latest interest was *ALfheim Online*, or *ALO* for short.

In that game, she turned into a fairy with transparent wings on her back, flew through a colorful, beautiful fantasy world, and fought monsters and fairies of other races with swords and magic.

ALO was the first game Karen ever tried, specifically so she could play with Miyu. Unfortunately, it was also a game that she instantly hated, because the random avatar she got upon starting it up was at least as tall as she was, setting off her personal trauma.

Incidentally, in VR games, real-life and avatar gender would always be the same, unless there was an extremely rare system error. A female player was practically never a man.

In *ALO*, Miyu played as a beautiful sylph, a wind fairy, by the name of Fukaziroh—an odd choice, given that it sounded rather manly. It was inspired by the name of Miyu's family's dog.

How did the dog get that name? When Miyu was young, her friend's dog had puppies, and when Miyu asked her parents to let her keep one, they kept refusing, using the word *fuka* ("not allowed"). And because the puppy was male and their old pet bird was named Tarou Shinohara, they attached the ending *jirou*, meaning "second son."

Miyu loved her childhood dog, Fukajirou, who'd died of old age last year. She'd decided to use his name as inspiration in VR, to keep his memory alive.

Karen didn't want her parents hearing them talk about VR games, so the two decided to go somewhere else to chat. They settled on a familiar old karaoke place they'd often visited in high school, and they had a long, fun conversation about Squad Jam.

Miyu had already seen the footage of Llenn winning the event. "Oh, man! You were fighting like a beast in there! Such carnage! It was awesome! I knew it was worth teaching you how to play! That was the best!"

She was absolutely over the moon and asked every question that came to her mind about the battle. Karen decided to tell her about everything, even the very fishy stuff about Pitohui and M—making Miyu swear to secrecy, of course—from how they'd met to what had happened in the event to Pitohui and M's apparently close relationship in real life.

"Hmm. Well, trust me when I say there are plenty of weirdos in VR games. As long as your actual name and address don't get doxed, you shouldn't need to worry, though!" Miyu said, reassuring her. Karen wasn't worried about that happening, so she was relieved for the moment.

For Miyu's part, she had invested a lot of time in *ALO*. She'd buffed up Fukaziroh an impressive amount, and she had an incredible sword to match. When combined with her odd and memorable name, she was building a major profile within the *ALO* community.

"There are always people ahead of me, of course. Sometimes they're just amazing. A little while ago, someone was looking for duel partners, wagering an eleven-part Original Sword Skill. She was unbelievable."

Karen didn't fully grasp the fun of battle in *ALO*, where characters could fly and use magic as well as fight with swords, but she certainly understood the concept of there always being someone better out there.

Fukaziroh had recently saved up enough yrd (the currency in *ALO*) to buy her own guild building—just a little shack. That would allow her to safely store her items there, so if she wanted, she could securely transfer her character over to a different game without losing progress.

Miyu had taught Karen about the conversion system, where a user with one ID could bounce around between any number of VR games, with their strength levels adjusted to relatively similar amounts between titles. Items and money did not carry over, however. You needed a place or a trustworthy friend if you wanted to keep them in your old game.

Miyu had that covered, at least, so if she wanted to, she could visit Karen in *GGO* whenever.

"But I think I'll be in *ALO* for the time being!" she said. "I mean, you're not going to leave *GGO*, are you, Kohi? Llenn's too tiny and cute for that!"

Yes, she is! No one will ever take my adorable daughter away from me! Karen thought, like a stubborn father.

Then she brought up the topic of Elza Kanzaki. Miyu had been a huge fan of Elza's ever since her debut and was dying for the chance to see her in concert in Tokyo. The last performance had been on the day of Squad Jam, and once Miyu hadn't won the lottery for concert tickets, Karen had decided to enter the tournament instead.

"I wonder when her next show is? It sounds like she's taking it easy right now. She hasn't updated her blog—says she's overseas. But it's not that big of a label she works for, right? No real info from their staff. Well, I guess we have no choice but to sing for her!"

Karen wasn't sure why they had no choice—but sing Elza Kanzaki songs they did, for as long as their booked time and lungs would allow them.

✳   ✳   ✳

Between spending time with Miyu and her other friends from high school and staying away from the bustle of Tokyo and the gunpowder stench of *GGO*, Karen's spring vacation passed in peace and quiet.

Eventually, March arrived.

On Wednesday the fourth—when the new semester was still far off for college students, and spring a ways away from Hokkaido—Karen went online with her laptop after lunch and saw that she had a message from *GGO*.

Curious, she opened it and found that it was just a standard Zaskar newsletter, the kind every player could elect to receive.

But the contents shocked her.

The message announced a second upcoming Squad Jam event.

Second Squad Jam.

Also known as SJ2. Ess-Jay-Two.

The event would happen in exactly one month, on Saturday, April 4th, 2026. One PM.

This, too, was a personally sponsored event, but rather than the writer from the last time, the donor was anonymous.

The basic rules were the same as the first Squad Jam, but with some minor alterations, so it would be necessary to consult the link for the full rules.

They were still determining the grand prize and would announce it before the end of the registration period—which was effectively open now.

Noon on April 1st was the deadline. If more than thirty teams signed up, there would be a team-against-team preliminary round starting at eight o'clock the night before the final. However, any team that included one of the leaders of the four highest-placing teams of the previous event would automatically be seeded out of the preliminary round.

That would apply to the fourth-place SDF(?) team of professionals, the third-place skull-logo team, and the runners-up of Saki and her high school gymnastics team.

And her.

Llenn, the champion.

What a stunning turn of events.

There really would be a second Squad Jam. And it was just next month.

Karen was staring at the screen in a daze when a gunshot sound effect went off, alerting her to another message. Yes, the game's default message-notification sound was a gunshot. It was both perfectly apt and totally obnoxious. At least players could change it.

Who could this one be?

Is it...Pito? Another order to participate? What will I do? Do I accept or refuse? If I do play, what will I do about what happened in the last one? Ask her about it? Hear her out? Ignore it?

She opened the message, heart racing, only to find that it was from Saki.

The message header was *Did you see the official message? They're holding SJ2!*

Yep, she'd seen it.

The body of the message continued, *Of course, all of us are in! No question about it! We've been training for this! And our tests are over! Spring break's almost here! It's a good thing they'll seed us out of the prelims! If you change your mind and decide to play, we'll all be overjoyed! We want to see you pumped up and ready for action! We wanna fight you! We wanna shoot you! We wanna battle to the death! PS: We wanna eat snacks, too! Invite us over again!*

It was a very excitable message, made somewhat more alarming by all the references to shooting and killing. At the very least, she could tell how pumped up Saki and her team members were.

But personally, Karen wasn't feeling it.

"I don't think I need to play…"

For one thing, she didn't have a team to join. She was perfectly capable of reaching out to Pitohui or M to set up a team again, but as was obvious from recent history, she didn't feel like doing that.

Of course, if they reached out to her…then she'd have to see how she felt.

At the current stage, she was not proactively considering participating in SJ2.

And with that conclusion in her head, she stopped thinking about it for the time being.

✳   ✳   ✳

About ten days later, spring break was humming along, and after all the time she could want to spend with Miyu, Karen finally flew back to Tokyo on Sunday, March 15th.

She was eager to get back, not just to prepare for the new school year and enjoy the cherry blossom viewing in Tokyo for the first time in her life, but mostly because she hadn't played *GGO* in a while.

"It's been so long since I shot a gun…"

She wanted to be tiny Llenn again.

Her flight was an extremely early one, to the annoyance of her parents—it touched down in Tokyo before ten in the morning. She rushed back to the entrance to her building, suitcase rolling behind her, excited about diving back in as soon as she got into her apartment.

She pulled out her keycard at the entrance of the high-rise apartment building, bowed to the familiar security guard, and disappeared beyond the sliding doors.

"…"

Which someone witnessed through binoculars.

Across the street from the building, in a parking garage about two hundred yards away, there was a German luxury SUV along the wall, the rear window lightly tinted. If you didn't get extremely close, you'd never notice that the person sitting there was holding a large pair of binoculars.

The person rotated the platform attached to the inside of the car window with suction cups. The binocular lenses rotated with it. A new target was acquired: a room on the fifteenth floor of the high-rise. The movement was crisp and practiced.

Two minutes later, the curtains on the apartment's window drew apart. The glass door slid open, and the resident appeared—a tall woman standing at about six feet.

Three minutes after that, the room sufficiently aerated, the glass door shut. And despite it being morning, the heavy curtains closed.

The person in the car pulled away from the binoculars, opened a laptop, and booted up a program. The logo that appeared said *Gun Gale Online.*

Then the mystery person lay down in the back seat, promptly put on an AmuSphere, and full-dove directly into *GGO* from the car.

"Link Start."

*   *   *

"Found it! I'll buy this one, mister! Right now! Insta-buy!"

Little Llenn, appearing in her dark-brown robe in *GGO* for the first time in many days, found what she was looking for.

"Yes! Yes! Yes! Yesssss!" she celebrated, like a rambunctious child.

She'd been checking out back-alley gun shops, and it was at the third of these that she'd found what she'd wanted to buy: a strangely shaped submachine gun.

Yes, it was the Belgian-made FN Herstal P90. The exact same model as her trusty partner, which had given its life to protect her during Squad Jam. Obviously, she wanted it customized on the spot. She had it, like her battle outfit and gear, painted dusty pink.

This was the second generation of P-chan, although it was impossible to tell the difference between them. What should she call it? P-chan Mk. II, or P-chan the Second?

They were both too wordy; just P-chan would do fine. She equipped the sling she'd used with the first one, hung it carefully from her shoulder under her robe, and headed out into the sci-fi world of tall buildings and gleaming neon.

Did winning Squad Jam turn her into an in-game celebrity, with people recognizing and hailing her on the street? The answer to that was no.

She was still hiding herself under her heavy robe, of course, but the only reactions she got, like before, were due to her size. Clearly, the scale and infamy of Squad Jam and the Bullet of Bullets were miles apart.

But she liked it that way.

She skipped happily down the street. Just getting the P90 was enough, so her plan was to do a little shooting practice, no battle, before logging out to the real world. She headed for the major mall that had a nice big shooting range.

"It's so fun to shoot my P-chan! Nine hundred shots a minute!

Showers of cartridges! Oh, what a lovely sound!" She hummed a creepy little impromptu tune because there was no one around to hear her.

Given how elated she was, it was no wonder she never noticed the avatar with the slender, boyish appearance who had been following her ever since she started her shopping excursion.

*   *   *

Monday, March 16th.

It was just the start of the week for the rest of the world, but Karen was still enjoying her long college spring break. The sky above was gloomy and dark.

This was a good day for her to clean at last, after which she got the packages she'd shipped to her apartment from her parents' house.

"…I'm bored."

There was nothing for her to do, and it was only just after noon.

She considered diving into *GGO*, but then she said, "You know what? I'd rather not…"

The day before, she'd decided she was "just going to practice shooting," and then she got the itch at the shooting range and chose to venture outside—"just to one of the easy environments"—for monster hunting. She'd ended up playing for nearly four whole hours.

Of course, there were other things besides playing games that she could do around the house, like studying for school, reading books, listening to music, or some combination of the above. But she had other ideas.

"I think I'll go for a walk."

Despite the poor weather, she decided to walk around the area. She even brought a folded-up shopping bag so that she could run an errand or two.

She shut the curtains, turned off the lights, took the elevator down to ground level, and left the front entrance.

"The park would be nice."

She headed for a nearby park, a beautifully verdant place. It was the middle of the day, and there were a fair number of people around, so Karen wasn't paying any attention to what was happening around her, and she failed to notice that ever since she'd left the apartment, a man had been following her.

After walking for an hour or so, then stopping at the supermarket and buying some groceries, she headed home.

Karen walked through a narrow alley. It was the shortcut she often took on the way home from one of the nearby train stations, with an apartment building wall on the right and small industrial lots on the left.

She would never walk there at night, of course, but it was only three o'clock. She took wide steps with her long legs, so ultimately she was moving at a good pace.

A young woman with two children on an electric bike came riding the other way, so Karen moved out of their path. The woman nodded her head and passed onward.

As she turned to watch the woman go, Karen finally noticed that there was a man standing directly behind her, about thirty feet away—watching her.

Karen hadn't realized someone was behind her and going the same direction, so she was startled. She stared at him.

Her first impression was positive: *He looks like an actor.*

The man was about five foot nine, not incredibly tall (and shorter than she was), but on the tall side for a Japanese man. His figure was beautiful, with long legs in jeans, a white T-shirt worn beneath a leather jacket, a broad chest, and tight, athletic muscles.

Even his face was impressively handsome. His glare was a bit mean but not to an extent that she'd call scary. Karen put his age at late twenties. His hair was black and grown out enough to reach his shoulders in long waves, though she didn't know if the effect was natural or artificial.

She turned and faced forward again. It wasn't polite to stare at others, even if they happened to be well-built and attractive. She started walking again, taking long steps to get back home.

Four minutes later.

"..."

Karen once again realized that the man was still thirty feet behind her.

She could actually see her apartment building just ahead. She was waiting on the other side of the street, at the crosswalk, when the man entered her sight again, and she realized he was continuing to follow her.

Okay, now this is scary...

Her caution mode jumped up a level. Just because she was taller than most men already didn't mean that a young woman like Karen was going to let her guard down around an unfamiliar man. She'd made a series of rather complex turns since the alley where she'd first spotted him, so this was clearly not a coincidental direction, but a sign that he was following her.

If it had been night right then, she would have taken some kind of protective action—hailing a cab or calling someone on her phone as she walked. On the other hand, if it had been night, she wouldn't have been walking this way regardless.

She tried to reassure herself that it was daytime, the street was large and busy, and her apartment was very close. When the signal turned green, she began crossing the street. Her destination was to the left on the other side, so after a bit she glanced to the side without turning her head.

The man crossed the street and turned left behind her. *Ugh, he's still following...*

It was obvious now. He was trailing Karen. Where had it started? The supermarket? Ever since the park? There was no way to know at this point, but if he'd been behind her the whole way, the thought was horrifying. That positive impression due to his good looks suddenly plummeted.

Time to get home.

Karen practically scrambled the last hundred yards to her building. She played it cool, suppressing her urge to sprint. There were plenty of cars on the street, as well as passing pedestrians and bicycles, so she didn't think he would attack her in the open, but a chill ran down her spine.

If this were *GGO*, she'd spin around and draw her knife, but in real life that would only earn her a quick trip to the slammer.

The entrance to her building required a keycard that only residents owned. Once she got in the first door, she would enter the front lobby, with an on-duty concierge woman and a male security guard.

If the man tried to follow her through the door, Karen would scream, and that would hopefully solve the problem. But once she allowed herself enough sense of relief to recognize this, the extra brainpower it freed up allowed her to consider another possibility. A much worse one.

If I go inside, won't I just be giving away my address?

If the man had seen Karen somewhere and followed her here, then if she used her key, it would tell him that she was a resident of the building.

What if he was following her to learn where she lived?

Ooh, who's that chick? Tall but hot. Where does she live? I gotta follow her there and find out. Then I can wait for her at the entrance every day and stalk around after her, heh-heh-heh...

The thought was so frightening that she had to force her imagination to shut down.

Her entrance was just ahead. Would she walk right in, or pass by it so that he didn't find out where she lived? That was the big question.

But where would she go if she passed the door? Find another business to kill time in? What if he kept following her? What if he was a real bona fide stalker, the kind that was obsessive and persistent?

Oh my God, what do I do what do I do what do I do what do I—?

As her brain threatened to overheat from panic, she heard a voice say, "Are you Karen...Kohiruimaki?"

"Yes, that's my name," she said, stopping and turning like a damn fool. There the man was, right in front of her face. "...Hya—!"

After a brief moment in which her mind went blank, she started to scream. But the man cut her off just in time.

"Please don't scream! It's me, Llenn! It's M!"

When in the how in the why in the hell?

Karen was still very confused.

Now she stood in the viewing room of her apartment building. The thirtieth floor of the building was a shared space that any resident could use. It was like a lobby, with large windows in the corner of the building, with tables, sofas, and vending machines that sold drinks.

It was only full on days when there were distant fireworks shows, and it was otherwise never really used. It often made you wonder why they had installed it in the first place.

The only people among the neatly lined-up sofas and tables were Karen and the man.

A few minutes earlier, right outside the front door of the building, the man had said, "Please don't scream! It's me, Llenn! It's M!"

Karen had stopped, startled. "Huh...? No way!" she'd yelled.

A woman passing on a bike at that exact moment jolted in surprise and lost her grip on the handlebars. The bike wobbled but didn't fall over.

Still, she couldn't help but yell about it. *This* was the man who controlled her combat partner in Squad Jam? The huge, buff bodybuilder?

She couldn't believe it.

Not because the avatar and player looked different. That was fine. She was the six-foot-tall skyscraper woman who played as a sub-five-foot girl. No, the problem was something else.

"Assuming you're M's player," she said, "how did you know I was Llenn? How did you find that out?"

The only people who knew that Llenn was Karen Kohiruimaki, or the other way around, were Miyu and the high school gymnastics team. She'd met M only twice, inside *GGO*, so there was no way he should know.

Of course, asking that question was actually admitting she was Llenn, but Karen was too confused to realize that in the moment.

"I'll explain that later. I came to see you in person, Karen, because I have a very important topic to discuss. This isn't the best place for it, so if possible, I'd like to go somewhere else, where we can relax and not worry about who might see or hear us," said the man who claimed to be M, his attractive features dead serious.

Karen stared at him as though he were a scammer. "And if I refuse?"

The man immediately replied, "On the night of April fourth, the second Squad Jam, someone is going to die."

It was impossible to believe but also impossible to ignore.

"If you try anything, I'll scream!" she insisted, taking him to the viewing room. Obviously, she wasn't going to invite him into her own apartment, and she doubted there would be anyone in the viewing room—a guess that turned out to be accurate.

It was also the tallest building in the area, so up on the thirtieth floor, nobody could see you unless you were standing right at the window.

So what in the world was going on that would lead to someone's death? Karen was still confused.

As soon as they entered the room, she went to buy some tea from the vending machine in the hope that it would calm her down. Instead, the man barged in and pressed his smartphone to the machine, paying the fee.

"It's on me. It's the least I can do to repay you for hearing me out."

"Well…thanks."

She tried drinking the tea, but it didn't taste like anything. It wasn't having the desired effect.

The man who claimed to be M bought a can of black coffee for himself and drank it with great relish. Maybe he was feeling a sense of accomplishment, since he'd convinced her to hear his story.

Karen let out a long breath and asked, rather awkwardly, "Are you…are you really M's real-life player?"

He'd been very polite to her, but she wasn't in the mood to return the favor to a suspicious man coming from out of the blue, so her tone of voice was less than kind.

"Yes," the man said, handsome and completely serious. That wasn't enough for her to trust him, of course, so ignoring whether or not this was rude, she asked, "Do you have any proof?"

"I don't," he said immediately.

"Huh? Then how do you expect me to believe…?"

"I can't show what I don't have. I can't lie to you."

This was getting a bit silly. She decided to offer him a suggestion that might work. "You could say something that only M and I talked about during Squad Jam…"

The battles in Squad Jam were aired, but unless you intentionally faced one of the cameras and shouted, they didn't pick up the audio of conversations. So only Llenn would know anything that M had said to her during the event.

But the man simply said, "That's not proof of anything. I could tell you, 'Llenn said this to me during Squad Jam,' but that might just be a story M told me."

"…"

Yes, that was a good point, but it also didn't make sense for the person who needed to prove himself to say it. This was becoming rather annoying.

"So really, the only way this will work is if you believe what I say, Karen."

"That's horrible!"

"I'm well aware."

"..."

She wanted to blow him off and go back to her room, but something stopped her; she couldn't ignore the claim that someone was going to die on the day of SJ2. Actually, something else was bugging her, too.

"Let's say for argument's sake that you *are* M... Can I ask you something? I mean, I'm going to."

"Be my guest."

"How did you know my name was Karen Kohiruimaki and that I'm Llenn? How did you know this was my address? That doesn't make any sense at all!"

In online games, it was possible to give away too many hints through conversation and attitudes that might expose you IRL, or in other words, to allow someone to piece together your real identity.

Pitohui often taught Llenn harsh lessons about this. *"Be careful what you say! Is it something you really should be telling a stranger? Is it?"*

What happened last month should have been the perfect example.

Saki had realized that Karen was Llenn. Karen hadn't believed it at first, but she'd figured out that Saki was Eva. They'd given each other plenty of hints.

Karen's hints were that she was in a desperate mood to do something to blow off steam on the day of Squad Jam and the fact that she'd placed a pink P90 key chain on her schoolbag—the exact sort of thing an ordinary girl in college did not bother with.

Saki's hints were that she was the leader of a gymnastics team that was good at catching and throwing things and that her nickname was Boss.

So what kind of hint had Karen given this man? Putting aside the fact that her real name was the basis for her character name (though not a straightforward match), there had to have been some hint that had allowed him to identify her last name, appearance, and address.

She couldn't think of what it was.

"Hang on... Do you work for Zaskar?" she asked out of the blue.

There was certainly a slim possibility of that. The developers of the game would possibly be able to identify her name and address just based on the user ID and e-mail address she'd submitted to them. And in fact, Karen had submitted her personal info to Zaskar in order to receive her Squad Jam prize.

But the man shook his head. "I don't."

"Then how? How did you learn my address and name?"

"..."

He was silent for several seconds.

"I can't tell you now. But I'll explain later," he said.

Karen wished she had a truth serum in her pocket. Or at least a gun she could point at his throat.

"But I want you to listen to what I have to say. It's important. It's very, very important."

"Well, I can't stop the sound from hitting my ears, so you might as well go ahead." Karen sighed, giving in. "But wait—before that, who are you really? What's your legal name?"

She didn't like the fact that he knew her full name, but not the other way around.

"Oh, I'm so sorry. I owe you that much. My name is Goushi Asougi. Goushi is written with the characters for *powerful* and *aspirations*, and Asougi is the same as the special word for *an impossibly huge number*. It's written with the same *A* character from Mount Aso, the character for *priest*, and *gi* from the Gion district of Kyoto."

This explanation came so naturally to him that Karen felt it couldn't be an alias—unless he was just completely used to this particular alias.

"Okay, Goushi Asougi. And which name should I call you?" she said politely, dripping with sarcasm.

"Either one is fine," he admitted.

Annoyed, she said, "Well…it's real-life manners to call you by your real-life name, so you'll be Goushi to me…"

That way, at least she knew that if anything funny happened, she could report him to the police under the name Goushi Asougi. The last name was rare enough that she could remember it easily. Officer, this is the guy. Setting aside the possibility that it was an alias.

Goushi pointed his handsome face directly at her and said, "Karen, please help me."

"…"

Karen did not react to this. She just listened, her expression a blank mask.

"There is something that only you, out of everyone in the world, can do."

What the hell is this? A pickup line?! she thought. She did not say that aloud.

"And if you don't help me…"

Then what?

"…then two people will die."

Why? Who? How?

"One of them is me. The other is Pitohui—in real life."

"What do you mean?!" snapped Karen at the mention of Pitohui's name. "Goushi, in the middle of the last Squad Jam, you said something about Pitohui killing you in real life! Is this continuing on from that?"

"That's right. Didn't I tell you that Pito was crazy?"

"…Yes. While you were blubbering with tears running down your face."

That was an image she really didn't want to remember: a big tough macho man weeping like a baby.

"Pito's taking part in SJ2. Along with me and the other people she's rustling up."

"And you want me to be on the team?"

Aha! It's finally making sense!

So the general idea was this. Llenn hadn't indicated that she would participate in SJ2 yet. If she joined Pitohui's team, they would be seeded past the preliminary round, thanks to her presence. And he was coming to ask her for that.

On the other hand, it couldn't possibly be that simple, she chided herself. There was no way he'd undertake this kind of stalking for such an ordinary reason. All he had to do was send a simple message. The prelims would be easy. And this nonsense about Goushi's and Pitohui's real-life personas dying was baffling.

"Wait...no," she said. "Sorry, continue."

"Okay. We're not asking for Llenn to be on our team this time. And at the risk of arrogance, we're not particularly worried about the preliminary round, anyway."

"I didn't think so. Any team put together by you and Pito is going to be tough. Probably good enough to win it all."

The only reason she included the word *probably* was because of Saki's team. SHINC had been formidable opponents last time. They were gearing up again and would certainly be contenders to win. (On a side note, Saki had told her that SHINC was an abbreviation of *shin-taisou* club, or "gymnastics club.")

Who would win between Pitohui's team and Saki's team?

Karen didn't intend to take part in SJ2, but she was interested enough to consider diving that day so she could watch the event unfold from the tavern. But for now, she still needed to hear out Goushi.

"Pito's entering SJ2 to win it, of course. Anything less than victory is the same thing to her, no matter what place we come in."

"That sounds like her."

"So what she's saying now is...if she doesn't win this, she'll die."

"Huh?"

"Pito—er, Pito's real identity—is saying, 'If I don't win SJ2, or if I get killed in the game, I'm going to commit suicide.'"

"..."

"And I'll die, too. If I don't kill myself, she'll kill me first."

"..."

"And when she says she'll do something, she means it."

"...Like when she threatened you last time and said she would kill you?"

"Yes," he said, much to her disgust.

The problem that arose in the first Squad Jam was going to be a thing again this time?! She recalled the image of the HK45 hand-gun pointed directly at her head, the way it shined in the light. It was still very vivid.

If Karen hadn't dodged that shot, her hair might still be long today. But she had gotten away and interrogated him at the other end of her P90, where he'd told her how crazy Pitohui was.

She hadn't really understood him then, and she still didn't. But the actions she'd taken out of sheer frustration had resulted in a clean ending, in which M hadn't died. Here was his player, alive and well. That was assuming this was really him, of course—but after all the conversation so far, Karen no longer believed he might be an imposter.

Given the rise in mentions of "death" and "killing," Karen felt self-conscious enough to glance around the area. If someone came into the room, she'd hear the door, but she checked all the same. This wasn't a conversation they could have around strangers. And she wasn't going to bring Goushi into her apartment, either.

"Goushi..."

"Yes?"

"Why would Pito place such bizarre conditions on you? Why would she suggest that if she dies in the game, she needs to kill herself or other people...?"

Karen stopped just short of asking *Is she crazy?*

"What did I tell you during Squad Jam? She's crazy. She's nuts. Her mind is enslaved by the concept of death, and she can't get enough of staking her life on any contest."

"…"

Karen wasn't sure if she should ask the reason why. But she wasn't going to get anywhere without doing so. Hoping that Goushi didn't actually know the answer, she asked, "Why is that?"

He answered her question with one of his own.

"Do you know about *Sword Art Online*?"

CHAPTER 3
SAO Loser

SECT.3

CHAPTER 3
SAO Loser

"Do you know about *Sword Art Online*?" Goushi asked.

"Of course," Karen replied instantly. She couldn't *not* know.

Sword Art Online, aka *SAO*.

The world's first VRMMORPG (virtual reality massively multiplayer online role-playing game), which had launched on November 6th, 2022, four years ago. The demonic game that trapped about ten thousand of its players inside of their dives before that very day was even over.

Akihiko Kayaba, the genius creator behind *SAO*, set up a horrifying trap within his game. It prevented players from logging out, and if their in-game characters died, or if someone in reality tried to force them out of the dive, the first-generation home VR game console known as NerveGear would instantly fry their brains with an ultra-high-powered signal pulse. It turned a simple game into a matter of life and death.

Kayaba presented players with only one means of survival: to beat the game.

Karen didn't know much more than the broad outlines of what happened. Over two long years, the trapped players eventually beat *SAO* and returned to consciousness in the real world.

But not all of them did. From what she'd heard, nearly four thousand players died over the course of that time. The ones who did make it out were labeled *SAO* Survivors, just like those who escape death in any natural disaster or event.

SAO was a true game of death, a high-stakes environment where if you died in the game, you died for real.

"Oh!"

She was wondering why Goushi would bring that up, until a theory popped into her head.

If Pitohui was obsessed with death and wanted to put herself into a competition that needlessly risked her own life, could that mean...? If so, it would certainly explain how tough she was and how close to death her mind existed.

Earlier, Pitohui had told her that she'd been playing VR games *since before the* SAO *Incident ended.* Could she have been talking about *SAO* itself?

"Please, just tell me honestly," Karen pleaded. "Is Pito...an *SAO* Survivor...? Did she undergo terrible experiences for two years in that game...and come out mentally scarred as a result... and still can't get over the act of having to risk her life in everything she does?"

"No," Goushi said, firmly shaking his head. "That's not the case. Pito isn't an *SAO* Survivor."

Oh. So she's not doomed to carry a cursed fate on her shoulders, Karen thought, relieved. But Goushi's next words caused her mind to sharpen again.

"It's the opposite. Completely the opposite."

"Huh?" She didn't understand. She needed clarification. "What do you mean, 'opposite'? How so?"

"Pito's the opposite of an *SAO* Survivor. I don't know if this term is even a real thing, but she's more like...an *SAO* loser."

"*SAO* loser...?"

"That's right," he said. His fashion-magazine-cover-model face looked straight at Karen. "This is jumping a bit ahead, but are you familiar with the terms *beta version* and *beta tester*?"

"Um...I think I might have heard them once before."

"Then I'll explain. Roughly speaking, a beta is a program that's still under development but is essentially playable and largely finished. So beta testers are the people who try out the beta to see how well it works. The beta test allows the developers to identify problem areas that they can improve in the final release."

"Okay…"

"*SAO* had a beta test before its launch, too. A thousand players chosen by lottery got the chance to play the world's first **VRMMO** before anyone else. They also got first priority on the initial sales run, so it was easy for them to be among those first ten thousand players."

Any person who was enthusiastic enough to sign up for a chance at a beta test would definitely pick up the final product on the day of release and boot it up that very day, Karen assumed.

She recalled when Miyu once said, *If I knew about* SAO *beforehand? You bet I would've found a way to get a copy. I'd have been right in there on release day. It's scary.*

Goushi continued, "But among the ten thousand lucky people who snagged the game, many had things to do in real life and couldn't spare the time to immediately start playing it on November sixth. They all had to reluctantly pass on logging in that first day and save it for later."

"So you mean…," she started to say, envisioning what an *SAO* loser would be, and checked with him to see whether she was correct. "Pito was a beta tester and had the launch edition, but she didn't get to play it when it started up…?"

This time, he confirmed her suspicions. "That's right. Pito was an *SAO* beta tester. She was one of the lucky thousand who wore her NerveGear and tore through that game like she was possessed. Naturally, she was dying for the chance to play the full game when it came out."

"But she didn't get that chance…"

"No. Through some trick of fate, there was something else she had to do that day. Something so important, so once-in-a-lifetime, it would decide the future course of her life. Pito cried her eyes out, but she wisely made that decision for her future. She would have to play *SAO* the next day."

Crying her eyes out because she couldn't play on the first day seemed like overkill—or an example of the incredible tenacity of game addicts. Karen didn't really understand it. Also, the way he was speaking about Pitohui made it seem like Goushi had actually been with her on that day.

Karen had to push these thoughts out of her head. "But thanks to that…she didn't get stuck in *SAO*, did she?"

"That's right. The moment the Incident started, nobody else could log in to *SAO* anymore."

"So…wouldn't that make her…lucky?"

"Ordinarily, you'd think so. But Pito was different. For years and years, she's had this fixation on death that she can't hide from others. Can you imagine how such a person might act when she's actually placed in a life-or-death game?"

"…"

Karen knew the answer, but she couldn't say it aloud.

"Would she be like a normal person and be terrified for her life?" he prompted.

"…"

"No, she wouldn't. Just the opposite. She would be delighted: 'I get to play the greatest game imaginable!' And what if she had that once-in-a-lifetime opportunity and missed out on it?"

"…"

"That night, after she got home from her incredibly important engagement and found out on the news that *SAO* had turned deadly, Pito flew into a rage. She cursed her fate that she couldn't be in there, screamed, wailed, cried, and raged. She even hurt herself, and when I leaped in to stop her, she knocked me out and broke three of my ribs and fingers."

"…"

Karen didn't even have the presence of mind to indicate that she was listening during his speech. His descriptions of Pitohui's actions were terrifying, but so was the matter-of-fact way he ran through them, despite the fact that they must have been painful memories for him, too.

"But there was nothing she could do about it. There was no way to get inside of *SAO* after that. She cried and screamed and raged, and after she got a bit of that out of her system, Pito dedicated herself to her work. Her rage at being an *SAO* loser transformed into success. Her new job took off, and now she's very successful at what she does."

"What does she do? Is she a company president or something...?"

Karen couldn't help asking, though she knew that it was taboo to do so. Goushi looked a bit surprised but said, "Yes, that's right. She's a president. And I'm an employee at her company."

Please don't tell me you're also her boyfriend, Karen silently willed. It worked, because Goushi didn't reveal anything more about his private life.

"VR games picked up again before the *SAO* Incident even resolved," he continued. "So Pito—and I, without any choice in the matter—played them whenever we weren't at work. Using her anger at being an *SAO* loser as fuel, Pito was demonically driven in each game she tried, but none of the games actually made you die, so they didn't get her blood boiling the way she truly wanted."

Um, you don't need or want your blood to boil. That'll kill you! Not to mention that dying means you can't play the game anymore, Karen thought, but she kept it to herself.

"And after two years of work and VR games, the *SAO* Incident came to an end," Goushi said, as if he were reporting on it. "Stories started coming out from the *SAO* Survivors about what they experienced within the game—and Pito exploded again. There are rumors that aren't officially confirmed but that everyone seems to accept as essentially being the truth: There were player killers in *SAO* who intentionally murdered other characters. In fact, there was a guild of them."

"...Huh?"

Karen's mind froze. She didn't understand what he meant at first. Slowly, her mind thawed and resumed thinking.

Inside of *Sword Art Online*, where any character's death caused the literal death of the player. Players PKing other players. But that meant…

"That's just murder!" she shouted, hoping he would say she was wrong.

"That's right," he said.

"…"

She had no words.

Goushi continued, his pleasant voice uttering the most unpleasant words. "Inside of *SAO*, the entire player population didn't band together as one for survival or completion of the game as quickly as possible. For some players, their sole motivation to keep going inside the game was to kill other players. Between the people they murdered and the self-defense of killing those murderers, a large number of the total players who died were killed by other players."

"I…can't…believe it…"

Until now, Karen had always just assumed that all the players who'd died in the *SAO* Incident had been killed by monsters. Or, in other words, that the architect of the Incident itself had killed them.

Instead, the players had killed *each other*. How did the *SAO* Survivors who had killed others, even out of self-defense, feel about that now? Karen had to force herself to stop thinking about it.

"I myself doubted the sanity of the player murderers, but Pito's reaction was completely different. She exploded like she did two years earlier. She destroyed everything in the house out of rage, including me."

"Um…in what way was her reaction different? Keep in mind I don't really want to know."

"You're starting to figure it out, Karen."

"Please don't tell me that. Well?"

"In both ways. She was frustrated because, in her words, 'If I was in *SAO*, I could've been a player murderer' and because 'I could've had the justification to kill those PKers instead!'"

"This is crazy...," Karen murmured.

"What did I tell you?" Goushi smiled—the first real one she'd seen from him. It was the kind of smile that, in public, would've charmed whatever woman he wanted. "Ever since then, Pito's mental state has been off the rails, but ironically, her work's been so overwhelmingly busy that she hasn't had the time to cause trouble for anyone else. While she might be crazy, she does possess a certain common sense and sociability. She's not capable of hurting others in real life and being a violent criminal. Except for me. I get beat up every day around her," he said with a grin.

"..."

Karen had no response.

"Like I said during Squad Jam, her mind's still trapped in that crazy *SAO* world. I thought she'd gotten it under control in the last few months... Playing *GGO* lets her kill other characters with guns and knives, which I thought released some pressure for her...but not getting the chance to join Squad Jam really brought it back in full..."

"Okay...I get it."

She didn't actually understand and didn't want to, either, but she said so anyway, because the general picture was clear enough. There was no evidence to back up any of this, so she couldn't categorically rule out that Goushi was lying about all of it, but Karen's experiences told her it was pointless to assume this.

Suddenly, she remembered very vividly what Pito had said when she'd invited Llenn to try out Squad Jam:

Listen, Llenn. If you ask me, you've got some problems you're dealing with in the real world... There's something in the real world that's got you down, huh? That's why you came to GGO—to blow off steam. Or more cynically, to escape your troubles... You're looking at me like, 'How did you know?' It's obvious. That's how it was for me, too! ...There's way too much stuff in the real world that gets me down or pisses me off, so I tear it up in here instead. I get to come in, guns blazing, and kill tons of monsters and people.

Ah, yes. Ah, yes.

With that image of Pitohui's gentle smile in her mind, Karen couldn't help but think, *Being too* tall *got me down? Big freakin' deal.*

Karen leaned toward the man across from her and said, "You claimed that Pito will get to take part in SJ2, so she's plotting to turn it into a game of life and death for herself, right?"

"That's right."

"And you want to stop her from doing that."

"That's right."

"So my question is…why didn't you take this problem of yours to someone else, like the police or a psychologist? Shouldn't they be way more capable of helping her than I am?"

She didn't want to say these things, but she had to. It was clear to her now that, in real life, Pitohui was dealing with some kind of madness, but Goushi should've understood this better than anyone. Why was he letting it fester? It didn't make sense.

"That's an easy question," he said, his tone of voice no different from before. "No matter how much it might help Pito, I don't hope for anything she doesn't want, either."

It took Karen several seconds to figure out what he meant by that. And despite grasping his point, she still had to be sure that he was okay with what he was doing.

"Pardon…? Is that supposed to mean that you, um, prioritize her wishes above all else?"

"That's right."

"Even if, as you admit, it's not perfectly…sane? Even if, God forbid, it ends in suicide?"

"That's right."

"…I don't understand you at all."

This is just off the rails, Karen decided. She knew Pitohui was a bit crazy, but now it was clear that Goushi wasn't entirely rational, either.

She picked up her now cold tea and drank it. Then she got up to throw away the empty can. She headed toward the trash can next to the vending machine along the wall, wishing she could just run straight out of the room. Instead, she tossed the can into the bin with a light clank.

When she turned back around, Goushi was right there—as though he suspected she would run. His thick arm reached out just past her head and slammed against the wall.

"Uh, what? Um... Well...well, er, this is...um..."

She looked right into the intense stare of Goushi's eyes, and with what little composure her mind still possessed, she realized, *Oh...this must be...that famous...wall-slamming mating ritual...*

Goushi glared at her and shouted, "Have you ever truly, passionately loved someone in your life? Have you ever been in love with someone you'd sacrifice your entire life for?"

She was so flustered that she couldn't have lied on the spot. Instead, as if she'd been given a truth serum, Karen answered, "I—I haven't..."

In a tapestry of emotions ranging from sadness to anguish to fury, the man yelled, "Then you have no idea how I feel right now!"

"Meaning...," Karen said, looking down at the man pressing her against the wall. "You're...in love...with Pito?"

"I love her!"

It was her first time ever experiencing the phenomenon known as the wall slam, and the fact that he was expressing his passionate love for a *different* person made it twice as strange. *You never know what life will throw your way,* she reflected.

"First of all...sit down. I'll hear what else you have to say. And I have a few questions of my own for you," she said. "Want anything to drink? I'll buy it."

*   *   *

Karen chose a powerfully carbonated beverage to keep her alert and bought another black coffee for Goushi.

"Here you go."

"Thank you. I actually don't like coffee. Especially black coffee. It does a number on my stomach."

"Um, do you understand how the Japanese language works?"

"I wasn't done yet. Pito loves coffee, though—especially black. That's why I drink it."

"…"

Love is terrifying, Karen groaned to herself.

They sat back down where they'd been a minute ago. She decided to ask what had been on her mind all along.

"Goushi, you were terrified of dying back during Squad Jam. I think that's a normal reaction, and I understand why you were so scared now. But you don't seem frightened about taking part in SJ2, where the same threat of death exists. Isn't that weird?"

"No, it's not. I'm not scared of dying after Pito's dead. I'm scared of dying and leaving her behind."

Oh, so they're both just that weird. I guess everyone has a soul mate out there. Once again, Karen kept this to herself.

Then again, maybe Goushi was the more rational one. At least he was looking for a solution to his problem. It was all so hard to figure out.

"Earlier, you said that I'd be able to help Pito, right? You wanted me to do that."

"Right. That's my business. It's why I'm here."

"So my question is, how am I supposed to help?"

"I want you to compete in SJ2 as Llenn. I want you to fight your hardest and beat Pito."

"Huh?"

"You need to beat her. I want you specifically to mercilessly slaughter her. That's how Pito can be saved. She won't commit suicide if you win against her. And I won't get killed, either."

"Wh-why?"

The solution to a person who claims they'll kill themselves if they die in SJ2 is to mercilessly slaughter them in SJ2? Is all that coffee doing funny things to your brain, Goushi? she wondered.

"Is all that coffee doing funny things to your brain, Goushi?" She couldn't hide her thoughts this time. She couldn't *not* say it.

"I'm well aware that my mind isn't exactly normal. But I doubt that's because of the coffee. I don't think they put that kind of stuff in coffee."

I wasn't looking for a serious answer to that question, she thought.

He continued, "But this is the only solution to the problem. I just want you to enter SJ2, find our team, and beat Pito. Naturally, she and I and our other members will do our best to stop you."

This sent Karen into a panic. "Huh? Wh-what? You mean I have to be your enemy the whole way? You aren't going to lull your team into a state of complacency to make it easier for me to beat Pito? I thought that's what you meant," she said, not a single thought spared for how cheap or cowardly someone might find this.

"That wouldn't make it much of a fair fight. It's cheap. It's cowardly. You can't do that. I'm going to fight my hardest."

This was the "help" he wanted for his solution to work. Was Goushi really the faithful hound dog? It seemed like his love was misplaced in certain key ways.

Her exasperation must have shown on her face.

"Please don't make that face," he said, looking handsome.

"I'm very sorry. I'm just having difficulty understanding a lot of this," she said, her voice dripping with irony. "Convince me, Goushi. How…? Why…? For what reason will me defeating Pito stop her from killing herself?!" she demanded.

In about thirty seconds, Goushi answered her question. He gave in to her demand.

And her reaction was *Oh. Got it.*

"All right…I'll enter SJ2! And I'll knock out Pito!"

Goushi gave her a gentle smile and said, "Thank you. You're my only hope," without a hint of self-awareness. Then he gave her an e-mail address that Pito wouldn't discover, and he left the viewing room.

"Oh! It's Karen! Hiii!"

"You're right. I didn't know she came up here."

It was Karen's four-year-old niece and her mother, Karen's older sister. They must have come in and passed Goushi right at the elevator. If they'd come twenty seconds earlier, they'd have seen Karen and Goushi alone.

Karen stammered, "H…hiii!" back, feeling a cold sweat break out over her. She said a silent thank-you to Goushi's fastidious personality for ensuring that his empty coffee cans were thrown away.

Her sister's apartment was on a floor higher than this one, so it wasn't clear at first why they would come down to this viewing lobby. But when her niece tottered over to the vending machine and said "Juice!" it clicked into place. This would be the closest drink machine.

Karen's sister tapped her phone to the machine and asked her, "What are you doing for the rest of spring vacation? We were planning on going for a little spring skiing. Interested in coming along?"

"Let's go skiing!" said Karen's niece.

It was a wonderful invitation, but Karen had lots of stuff to do by April 4th. She couldn't spare a single day for anything else.

"Oh, sorry. I already decided that I've got a ton of books to read over vacation," Karen said. It was a very weak excuse, but they didn't seem to see through it.

CHAPTER 4

SECT.4

Preparing for SJ2

CHAPTER 4
Preparing for SJ2

Back in her apartment, Karen peered at the calendar function of her computer.

It was March 16th. That left about two and a half weeks until April 4th, the day of SJ2.

Karen put together a plan to defeat Pito. She typed up whatever came to mind in the to-do portion of her scheduling app.

First, she needed to level herself—Llenn—up in *GGO*. "I've gotta get stronger…"

Llenn was an agile character, but that was honestly her only feature. While she'd emerged as champion of the first Squad Jam, good luck had saved her on multiple occasions. There was no guarantee she'd be that lucky twice.

So she'd do battle as often as time allowed, earning experience and credits, powering up her abilities and weapons, and adding skills (special abilities) that would be useful in battle.

She'd fought with a knife at the end of Squad Jam, and it had been a good reminder to her that she really needed a sidearm handy in case her P90 jammed or ran out of ammo.

The knife had gone back to M, so she decided to buy the same one. It was fairly expensive, so she'd need plenty of credits. But this wasn't a big problem. If she used every day of spring vacation left, she could get pretty far and earn plenty of money, too.

However, there was one issue she still had to solve—and before the April 1st deadline for submission.

"Who...should I team up with...?"

Squad Jam was a team battle-royale event. Llenn had a seeding advantage because she won the last one, but she still couldn't enter as an individual.

Someone. She just needed someone. Did she know anyone who would fight with her?

"..."

There was no one.

The only person she'd known in *GGO* before Squad Jam was Pitohui. She'd met M during the event, but M wasn't going to be on her team this time. He was her enemy now.

"Saki's team...is off-limits..."

After Squad Jam, she'd met Saki's gymnastics team, led by Eva. But they were a tight-knit, full team of six. They understood one another, helped one another, and fought as a cohesive team; it was what made them so tough.

She didn't want to ask one of them to leave that group so she could take their place, or have any of them leave to join her instead. Perhaps if she explained the situation, they would understand her plight—but she gave up on that idea. She couldn't burden high school girls with something like this.

"I guess I'll just have to find someone tough within *GGO* and seduce them onto my side..."

It seemed like the most realistic possibility. She'd just hang out on the streets of SBC Glocken and pick up guys by explaining that she was the winner of the last Squad Jam. "Hey there, pal, you look like a thick slab of meat. You feel like entering SJ2 with me?"

But would that actually work? And would anyone who accepted her invitation actually prove to be worth her while? Would they be good teammates? Or would they accept it if she said, *You're just here to fulfill the team requirement, and once the event starts, you can do whatever you want*?

"I'm guessing that won't work," she mumbled. The worst thing that could happen was if she signed someone up and then they decided to bow out on the day of the event.

Also, if they accepted the request to be on her team and fight seriously, what would they think of Llenn's insistence on going for only Pitohui? Llenn's goal in SJ2 was to kill Pitohui, not to win. In fact, if that worked out, she'd probably consider just resigning to get it over with. If they took each other down, that would work, too.

She needed someone trustworthy enough that she could confide in them and know they would understand and be reliable enough to guarantee their participation. If their character was powerful, even better.

Was there even a single person that fit the bill in this world?

No, there wasn't. Or if there was, she didn't know them. She had few friends.

"Ugh..."

Elza Kanzaki's crystal-clear singing voice cut Karen's groan short. It was coming from her cell phone, which was sitting on the charging base at the edge of her desk. Her ringtone.

Karen reached over with a long arm, lifted the phone, and glanced at the screen.

"Aha! There *is* someone!"

On the display was the name MIYU SHINOHARA.

Miyu had called to talk about the Elza Kanzaki mini-concert happening in Tokyo in mid-April. Instead, it was Karen who did all the talking.

In order to save the life of some complete stranger, a crazy lady who ran a company, she needed to kill that lady's character in the second Squad Jam. And she needed Miyu's help. Just convert over to *GGO* and enter SJ2.

Karen finished this plea with a heartfelt "I know this is asking too much, but there's no one else I can turn to for help. Please... please help me!"

Miyu replied, "Heh... I guess Fukaziroh's gonna kick some ass in *GGO* this spring... I'd better hold back so I don't totally let loose and kill this Pitohui chick myself..."

✳   ✳   ✳

Thus began the period of intensive training for Karen and Miyu, Llenn and Fukaziroh.

First, Miyu had to convert Fukaziroh from *ALO* to *GGO*. It was an easy process on its own, but when she told her sylph guild-mates in *ALO*, who would be holding her items for her while she was gone, they naturally asked her why.

"I'm going to enter a mini–battle tournament in *GGO* with my friend who won the last one!" Miyu briefly explained.

"Wow, that sounds fun! Hey, let us join, too!"

"Yeah! Let's go invade *GGO*!"

"We'll show them our fairy power!"

The rest of the gang started getting carried away. But this was an awfully large group to get involved in a matter of someone's life or death, and Karen hadn't explained to them how she was personally involved with the matter. Miyu had to take great pains to let her guildmates down.

The instant Fukaziroh converted over, Llenn was waiting for her at the starting point of *GGO*. In this game, that was a particular street corner of SBC Glocken, the capital city.

The sky was always red, like the atmosphere had gone out of whack, with buildings that stretched straight up into it, and shining metal ground that glowed with reflected neon light—a world that was at once austere and chaotic.

While the conversion system allowed for characters on a single ID to be transferred between games, the avatar's appearance was always fixed for each separate game. Karen had tried out a number of games, looking for a tiny avatar, until she found Llenn.

Fukaziroh had been a beautiful fairy with long, flowing hair. What would she look like in *GGO*?

Llenn was dressed in her brown robe, feeling her anticipation grow when molecules of light burst into existence and began to build a human form.

"Ooh!"

It was the first time she'd seen what it looked like when a new character was born into the world. Soon the light began to take on color and fixed into shape.

"Ohhh...oh? Ooh!"

A character was born before her sparkling eyes.

The character raised her head and blinked. "Yo, Kohi! Oops, I mean, Llenn!"

It was definitely Fukaziroh.

And in *GGO*—

"What's wrong? Does my face look weird?"

—she was a beautiful blond girl—

"No! You're really cute!"

—almost as short as Llenn was.

"Whoo-hee! That's...*me*?"

Fukaziroh in *GGO* was only a tiny bit taller than Llenn— perhaps just a tad under five feet tall. It was the kind of body that threw off the world's sense of scale, what with all the bodybuilders and lanky giants around.

Her hair shone a brilliant gold and hung down her back. Her eyes were a reddish brown, and her features were pretty but rather sharp on the whole, as though they might cut you if you touched them.

In terms of being pretty, short, and blond, she matched Milana from the gymnastics team, but they couldn't have seemed more different otherwise. If Milana was the kind of cute that made your cheeks dimple when you looked at her, then Fukaziroh was more like a demonic imp that raised your hackles. Perhaps *apprentice witch* was a better description.

"Nice, nice! Too bad I don't have much in the way of boobage, though!" Fukaziroh exclaimed, feeling herself up with both hands over the starter combat fatigues.

"Ooh! That's an F-8000 series, missy! You just started, so you've got no attachment to it yet, right? Wanna sell me the avatar along with your account? You can make a pretty decent chunk of cash!" said a broker who apparently did a trade in buying and selling rare avatars. He seemed like a real creep.

"Hmm, that's a real tempting offer! How much are we talkin', mister?" Fukaziroh asked.

She sounded like a teen girl haggling with a middle-aged man over the price of sex. Llenn promptly grabbed her and dragged her away.

Llenn and Fukaziroh crammed into a private room at a decrepit tavern to hold a planning session.

There were just too many things they needed to prepare in order to compete in SJ2 and actually beat the powerful Pitohui. First, they had to check out Fukaziroh's stats in *GGO*.

Conversion preserved the strength of the character in relative terms. So if a player buffed up their character to have high strength in the previous game, their converted character would appear with high strength in the new game. If Llenn was to convert to another game, she would still be very speedy and agile—even if she looked like a sumo wrestler.

In *GGO*, as with nearly every other VR game, a special gesture with the left hand opened up a floating game window. It was ordinarily invisible to anyone but the individual player, but you could elect to send the contents to another player so they could see it, too.

Fukaziroh sent over her character stats.

"Wha…? What…is this…?" Llenn gasped.

Strength, agility, durability (stamina), dexterity, intelligence, luck.

Out of the six main stats that were the basis for each *GGO* character's abilities, compared to Fukaziroh, Llenn was higher only in agility and dexterity. Her friend had her beat by a mile in every other one. Her strength and durability were especially high. That meant she could carry very heavy guns and gear around and would be able to stand up to plenty of shots.

She looked just like a fragile little girl, but her strength and stamina were nearly at M's level. She was practically a cyborg.

"Yeah, that seems about right," said Fukaziroh matter-of-factly, fiddling with her blond bangs. She wasn't surprised at all.

How much time had Miyu put into VR gaming? How many dozens—no, how many hundreds of hours? Llenn felt a chill run down her back. But at the same time, she couldn't help uttering the first thought that came to mind.

"You're gonna be a big help!"

Next up was getting together Fukaziroh's new *GGO* weapons and equipment. She'd come from *ALO* with nothing, only the clothes that every new character wore. Zero items. Cash…

"Um, a thousand credits."

"…Yeah, that's the starter amount."

She'd be able to buy one cheap pistol, and that was it.

"It's okay. No problem," Fukaziroh said.

"Yes problem!"

She wouldn't survive SJ2 like that. She needed the best possible gun. But Llenn didn't have all that much money, either. She'd just bought herself a new P90, after all. And she didn't have much gear to hand over. She'd sold the optical gun and her Skorpion submachine gun already.

That left no choice but fighting some monsters to earn credits, but that path would be a tough one since they had only two weeks to work with. It hurt that they had so little money despite their strength.

"Well…I guess I don't have any choice…but to dip into my

savings," Llenn murmured. *GGO* allowed you to buy credits with real money, using a bank transfer.

But Fukaziroh immediately protested, "No, I can't force you to do that! Listen, Kohi—I mean, Llenn. But we're talking about real money, so I guess it's Kohi? I know you get plenty of allowance from back home! But you're supposed to be saving that for when I come to Tokyo for the Elza Kanzaki concert and you buy me some ultra-fancy sushi in Ginza, right?"

"That was never on the table! But if we pull this off in SJ2, then I'll owe you dinner..."

"Yesss! I heard you say it! I'm the witness!"

"Okay then, Miyu—I mean, Fukaziroh. Geez, that's hard to say."

"You can just call me Fuka, like everyone else. Anyway, why don't you just ask for assistance from the person who was begging you to save this other person's life?"

"Ummm..."

That hadn't occurred to Llenn. She mulled it over now.

"I guess that's the only way..." Nothing else was coming to mind. M certainly played a good amount, and he might have·some credits and spare equipment gathering dust. It seemed worth a shot.

But she'd have to log out first. Goushi had given her his regular e-mail address. After all, there was a possibility that Pitohui might discover any correspondence or conversations they were having within *GGO*.

"Okay, I'll just explore this drab, colorless world, then! Let's see if I can break my record of getting hit on in a day!" said Fukaziroh, who was used to the colorful realm of *ALO*. She stayed behind while Karen logged out.

Karen then sent Goushi an e-mail explaining the situation and asked for help with gear and credits for her friend so they could pull off this SJ2 maneuver. However, she did make sure to request that he didn't spend a single yen on them.

His response came back in less than a minute.

He said that it was his request of her in the first place, so he wanted to help. He would set up an item box in town by a certain time. It wasn't an actual box, of course, but something you could touch that would transfer data. He also sent her the password to open it. Presumably, this intermediate step was to ensure that no record remained.

When Llenn dived back into *GGO*, she headed to the designated location with Fukaziroh, who was now wearing a robe to cover up her ostentatious looks.

"I got chatted up by forty-three people in just that amount of time! That's impressive! There really are barely any women in the game! It's like a harem for girls!" she said.

They found the present from M behind a trash can in an empty alleyway. Fukaziroh touched it and entered her password, and credits flooded into her empty wallet.

"Whaaat?" Llenn exclaimed.

"Ooh!" Fukaziroh marveled.

The number was enough to make them leap to their feet.

"Llenn…this isn't some mistake, right…?"

"I don't think so…"

"I'm not going to be asked to sell my organs later or do some commercial-tuna-fishing stint on the high seas, am I…?"

"I don't think so…"

Along with the vast sum of cash, M had left them a simple message.

This should be good for now. If you need more, let me know.

Fukaziroh turned to Llenn, dead serious. "I want to marry him right now. Give me his e-mail."

Their money problem had been solved. Next up was Fukaziroh's equipment. First, she needed her main weapon, the primary tool for attacking enemies.

"I've got the strength and stamina to equip even the heaviest weapons. I can do greatswords or battle axes, for example. I really like using long lances."

Those weapons didn't actually exist in *GGO*, and even if they did, they wouldn't be of much use. Llenn steered Fukaziroh to a good weapons dealer at the shopping mall.

So what kind of gun should she put in Fukaziroh's hands? Llenn thought it over and discussed with her friend; she came to the conclusion that the best thing to provide support for her speedy self would be a high-firepower gun.

Optical guns—aka ray guns, laser beams, or blasters—lost strength when they hit anti-optical defensive fields, so it was common knowledge that live-ammo guns were better against human opponents. In fact, almost everyone in both the BoB and SJ used regular guns.

Llenn showed Fukaziroh a variety of live-ammo weapons at the mall's weapon store. She checked out machine guns with high rates of fire that could suppress a wide area at once, and assault rifles with a good balance between power and size.

"It's not clicking for me," Fukaziroh commented, unimpressed. "They all look tough, but they're just not beautiful."

Well, the aesthetics aren't the issue here! Llenn wanted to say, but she couldn't—she had bought her first P90 on looks alone.

Fukaziroh's selection process was at an impasse.

"Well, darn…"

Llenn was at a loss. If only Pito or M were here, with all their extensive knowledge of guns. But that was obviously a lost cause. Without a better suggestion, they'd just have to keep looking.

"Let's go to another shop, Fuka."

"Okay."

They went from the mall to a little alley store like the one where Llenn had bought her P90.

In *GGO*'s setting, optical guns were used on the colony ships that humanity used to return to Earth. Live-ammo guns were used on Earth—either excavated from their original period or re-created with blueprints.

Nobody could craft weapons above middle tier. You had to go exploring in dangerous ruins and beat the bosses there or find and excavate them yourself. As the game went on, the developers introduced new weapons in various locations—a constant source of excitement among the player base.

These little hole-in-the-wall establishments dealt in the rarest and most powerful of weapons. And the very first one they walked into got Fukaziroh's eyes sparkling.

"Llenn! This one! What gun is this? It's supercool! It's beautiful! It's gorgeous! It's *magnifique!*"

"Huh? Which one?"

What gun had inspired this rapturous response from Fukaziroh? Llenn trotted over to her in excitement, feeling as if she were watching her old self buying that first gun.

"That one!"

She looked up at the gun on the shelf that Fukaziroh was pointing at.

"What's…this…?" Llenn said, her face twitching.

It's ugly!

Only the power of friendship could keep her from saying it aloud.

The object was exceedingly lame.

It was a bit over two feet from one end to the other, about the same length as a long submachine gun. It had a grip, a trigger, and a stock to press against the shoulder, so it had to be a gun. The metal was colored a shade of brown typically labeled "desert tan," with the grip and other features being black.

Wow, it truly was an incredibly ugly gun.

The worst feature of all was the bulge in the center. It was a rotating cylinder, like a revolver, but jutting out like the belly of some fat old man. The barrel was very thick and short, and also incredibly unfashionable and ugly.

In short, to Llenn, it looked like a very unfortunate cross

between a revolver and a submachine gun, with the sizes all wrong so that it looked very fat and dumpy.

"You don't know this one, either, Llenn? Well, I like it! This is what I want! What kind of gun is it?"

"Ummm…"

It was the first time Llenn had ever seen it, so the only description she could possibly give her friend was that it was an extremely ugly gun.

She read the tag attached to it. It said MGL-140. That had to be the gun's name.

But it didn't tell Llenn anything. What kind of gun was it? What bullets did it shoot?

Then the store clerk finished serving another customer and came over to the two girls. He was a young man wearing jeans, a T-shirt, and an apron with a United States Navy camouflage pattern on it.

He wasn't an NPC (non-player character) controlled by a computer, like the shopkeepers at the big mall. This was an actual *GGO* player who did business in the game to earn money.

"That's an automatic grenade launcher! It's the first one I ever saw, too! They just introduced them to the game, so folks started pulling them out of the ruins. Just got two in the other day!" he said with a friendly and welcoming smile.

"A grenade launcher. So this is what they're like," Llenn remarked. She knew what they were, but she'd never actually seen one.

"Gre…nade?" Fukaziroh didn't know much about modern weapons.

The sales clerk explained, "A grenade is basically a projectile that's packed with gunpowder so that it explodes. So a hand grenade, like the name suggests, is basically a bomb that you throw by hand."

"Ah, uh-huh."

Llenn let the sales clerk do all the explaining, since he was being very nice and thorough about it; he seemed to know more than she did.

"A grenade launcher is a gun that's designed to shoot grenades farther than you can throw them. It can shoot a 40 mm grenade about 1,300 feet at max power."

"Ooh! So it's not only cute—it's also powerful!"

"Yes, it is! And it's really fun to watch the way it arcs through the air! Normally, you need to load them individually, shoot the grenade, then remove the casings so you can load the next one—but this gun is different. You see that cylinder magazine? You just pack six grenades in there, and by a simple pull of the trigger, you can shoot two of them a second. Empty the whole mag in three seconds!"

"Oh-ho. You can rain destruction upon the enemy!"

"Indeed! Each detonation will spray shrapnel to a radius of about fifteen feet. Now imagine that happening six times. This is undoubtedly the most powerful grenade launcher in *GGO* at the moment!"

"Nice, nice!"

"There are many varieties of 40 mm grenades. In addition to the explosive kind, there are smoke-screen grenades, incendiary thermite grenades that burn at incredible temperatures, even flare grenades that come with parachutes that make them hang up in the air. There are many ways to play around with grenades!"

"This is sounding better and better!"

"And *GGO* even has fictional plasma grenades that don't exist in real life! Nothing feels better than tossing one of those off and seeing your enemies blasted!"

"Hya-hoo!"

It was almost like seeing a street-salesman routine right outside of a busy train station. Fukaziroh hopped and clamored, "Hey, pal! I'll take it! Sell it to me!"

Then the salesman lowered his tone of voice. "But it's expensive. Have you...taken a look at the price tag?"

As a matter of fact, they hadn't. Llenn glanced at it.

"Hrrrgh! Uurgh!"

She practically spit up blood.

As expected of such a powerful weapon, even the price tag was destructive. How many of her (not very cheap) P90s could she buy with this amount? That was a question she didn't want answered.

But at the moment, Fukaziroh was extremely wealthy, thanks to her private donor. "I'll take it! I'll take it!"

She fiddled with her window, showed the clerk the amount she was holding, and said, "I'll buy both of 'em! I wanna blast with one in each hand! And give me all the ammunition you've got for it!"

"…"

The clerk gave her a look like he'd never seen such an idiot, then recovered with a smile. "Th-thanks for your business! Oh, good… That'll pay next month's bills…"

Apparently, he was having trouble making ends meet. Llenn realized this was a good lesson for her: If finding a job turned out to be difficult, making a living off games wouldn't be any better.

So Fukaziroh got two MGL-140s and a pile of grenades to use with them.

"I wanna shoot 'em, I wanna shoot 'em!" she clamored.

Since the guns were so big, they had to go into her in-game inventory space.

A player's storage was like an invisible backpack. If you put an item inside of it, there was no need to hold that item. You couldn't put more than your carrying capacity in there, but Fukaziroh had such high strength that her capacity was vast.

"What about buying your other gear?"

"That can wait!"

"Fine. I want to see how powerful those things are, too. So do you want to visit the shooting range?" Llenn suggested.

"Don't be ridiculous! We're going out in the wilderness to do battle!"

A week had passed since Fukaziroh's arrival in *GGO*.

Thanks to M's investment, known to them as the M Fund, she had plenty of equipment. There wasn't a single sign left that she was actually a fresh-faced recent convert to the game.

After much deliberation, Fukaziroh's final gear loadout was as follows:

On top, a long-sleeved camo combat shirt. The pattern was something used by the American military called MultiCam, featuring various shades of brown and green. Over her shirt was a slimming green bulletproof vest. It had several pouches for more grenades. Brown gloves for her hands.

Below, she wore a pair of flared-bottom shorts that resembled a skirt, with the same camo pattern. Black tights covered the rest of her legs, which ended in short brown boots.

Her long blond hair was rolled up into a bun—which she stuck a hairpin into—at the back of her head. Llenn wondered where she'd found an item like that in the game; it turned out that she'd bought a tiny hand knife and had the store grind it down until it was small enough to serve as a hairpin.

And atop her head she wore a green helmet that was just a little bit too big.

The overall effect was of a girl who was getting into hiking. Miyu was much more skilled at the feminine things than Karen, so she put more effort into what she wore. Her clothes just happened to be camo patterned.

Then there was the pair of six-shooting MGL-140 grenade launchers, each one slung over a shoulder by a strap. She left them colored the way they came.

There was also a plastic holster on her right thigh holding a Smith & Wesson M&P 9 mm semiautomatic pistol, which she'd bought at some point. Apparently, that was in case twelve grenades weren't enough in a battle against monsters, and she needed to charge in shooting.

Llenn asked her how, well she was practicing shooting and received this answer: "If I get close enough, I can manage!"

On her back was a green pack. It was full of grenades. Her inventory, too, was full of spare grenades, right up to the limit she could carry. That was over a hundred in total.

"Shooting guns is fun, Llenn! C'mon, let's go!"

By the time she'd taken her guns out in search of powerful enemies, Fukaziroh had been fully committed to the *GGO* experience. While Llenn was still battling the pressure of needing to beat Pitohui, Fukaziroh seemed to have completely forgotten their actual mission.

Still, Llenn couldn't ask for anything more than a partner who was doing her best to get tougher. She worked with Fukaziroh, using the opportunity to improve her own character.

Under red skies, Fukaziroh scanned the horizon for monsters and popped off expensive grenades left and right. "Yahoo! Purify the corruption!"

The 40 mm grenades flew through the air and landed on the side of the target, the fuses lighting and setting off the detonators.

Even large monsters would blow up into chunks on a direct grenade hit—or at the very least, suffer major shrapnel damage on a near miss. Llenn would then dart in with superhuman speed and finish off the stunned creature with her P90. If ammo wasn't needed, a good stab to the back with her knife would do the trick.

They were already longtime friends. As teammates, they quickly settled into a very comfortable rhythm.

"Bullet circles are so handy to have!" Fukaziroh exclaimed. She'd already mastered *GGO*'s form of system assistance.

A bullet circle was the glowing green circle that only the shooter could see. It appeared less than a second after the character rested their finger on the trigger of the gun. Its size varied

depending on the type and quality of gun and ammo, distance to target, and character stats. It also fluctuated in size with the heartbeat of the shooter.

Once fired, the bullet would hit a random spot within the circle, so the shooter always wanted to fire when the circle was at its smallest. Naturally, when their heart rate rose with anxiety and excitement, it could be very difficult to get the best shot off.

Most normal guns and ones like Llenn's P90, which you pointed directly at the target, were quite straightforward to aim. So how would the bullet circle differ for a grenade launcher, which shot a projectile in an arc, similar to throwing a ball a long distance?

"Evidence over theory. A picture is worth a thousand words. In one ear and out the other," Fukaziroh said, handing one of her guns to Llenn and prompting her to use it.

"It's so heavy...," Llenn grunted. The MGL-140 felt like a block of lead. She couldn't possibly hold and fire it with one hand.

According to the real gun's data, the gun alone weighed over thirteen pounds and held six grenades that were over ten ounces each, so in total it added up to nearly twenty pounds when battle ready. It was quite a difference from the P90, which was only six pounds fully loaded.

The fact that Fukaziroh could lug two of these around with ease told Llenn a lot about her physical power.

"Okay, just one shot."

She clutched the grip below the barrel and held it in place with her lower back, rather than her shoulder, then touched the trigger of the MGL-140. A green circle appeared on the ground about two hundred yards away, tilted at a forty-five degree angle from where she pointed it. Tilting the barrel a bit higher caused the circle to move farther away.

She pulled the trigger, and with a cute little *pomp!* a black object shot forth, the recoil harder than she expected. The cylinder rotated one chamber to the right.

About three seconds and change later, the grenade exploded in the distance. A burst of dust and dirt shot up, and then the sound of the blast just a beat later.

She handed the MGL-140 back to Fukaziroh. "I get it now…"

It was indeed easy to aim. The clerk had said, *The real MGL-140 has a special angle-changing stock that you press against your shoulder, and it uses an optical sight to aim, but with the bullet circles in* GGO, *that's actually more of an annoyance, so you don't need it.*

Now that made sense to Llenn. Sure enough, Fukaziroh didn't have the laser sight on the MGL-140.

That cleared up the question of the bullet circle. "What about the line?" Llenn wondered. The counterpart to the bullet circle in *GGO* was the bullet line. It was a form of player assistance for the defender—a red line that could never exist in real life, displaying the trajectory a bullet was about to travel to the characters on its receiving end. The only exception to this rule was the first shot from a sniper whose location was unknown.

By watching the bullet lines carefully, *GGO* players could do what was essentially impossible in real life—actually dodge bullets.

Llenn wanted to see what the bullet line was like for herself, so she stood two hundred yards away and had Fukaziroh aim at her.

"Oh, I see now."

As she expected, the line followed a high curving arc. It reached down toward her at a diagonal angle from a great distance.

Using a phone-like communications item that Fukaziroh had bought for the two of them, Llenn said, "Okay, I get it. It's what I thought it'd be."

"Try some dodging practice, then. I'll shoot three," her friend said abruptly, and Llenn heard three quick shots, *pomp-pomp-pomp.*

"Hyaaa!" she shrieked, bolting into action. Three explosions happened in succession behind her. She felt the ground rumbling beneath her feet. A gust of air buffeted her back.

When she turned around, the ground was simply gone from where she'd been standing moments ago. The gun was frighteningly powerful. "Yikes…"

The grenade had to fly into the air and then down, leaving a few seconds between firing and detonation. In that sense, it was much easier to dodge than a typical bullet—but a grenade exploded and threw shrapnel. It wasn't at all like a bullet, where simply moving a foot or two put you in the clear.

After mercilessly unleashing those grenades, Fukaziroh's first words were "Mmm, nice. Good speed. Very impressive."

"It wasn't impressive! It was terrifying!"

"Yeah, but SJ2's going to be a lot more terrifying, right?"

"...Okay, you have a point," Llenn admitted as she returned to her friend.

"This is a fun weapon! It's so powerful! I'm glad I bought it! I'm glad he was selling it!" Fukaziroh was quite satisfied. Nonetheless, she added, "It's too specialized, though. I can't fight with these alone."

That was her VR gamer experience speaking—she said what Llenn was thinking before the words could leave her mouth. The multigrenade launcher had very impressive power, indeed. But it was a weapon with many different drawbacks.

For one thing, it was rare and expensive. Not the sort of thing you could easily buy.

It was also very heavy, with a high strength requirement. Only very advanced characters could use it, and its bulkiness made it difficult to combine with other weapons—except for buff characters like Fukaziroh.

And then there was the biggest downside: Once you fired all six grenades, it took a long time to reload.

To load up the MGL-140, you undid the latch and twisted the gun to expose the cylinder. Then you dumped out the shells, wound up the cylinder's spring with your fingers, and inserted new grenades before popping it back into place. No matter how well she performed it, the whole process was going to take Fukaziroh a good ten seconds each time. If she tried this out while fighting solo, she was going to get riddled with bullets.

"This is a gun that exhibits its best value from a support role in party play! I guess it's most similar to high-power attack magic with a long command."

"Well, I don't know how magic in *ALO* works...but maybe you're right."

"Yeah, it'd be a lot easier if you could fly...," Fukaziroh said wistfully. Everyone could fly in *ALO*.

"Now, now, young fairy. You're in the human world!" Llenn shot back, speaking like an old fogy.

"Hmph. Oh well! In that case, I'll blast 'em from the back row while you rush up close and attack, Llenn!"

"Got it! I'm so glad you're really tough now, Fuka! Also, since we're out here, there's one more strategy I'd like to test out..."

"Oh? Like what?"

* * *

Over spring break, Karen and Miyu continued diving into *GGO*. She had to power herself and her team up as much as possible by April 4th. Luckily, her college vacation had no strings attached.

Even still, Karen's limit each day was around six hours of playtime. Any more than that, and she got mentally exhausted. She'd never played that long before this. It was both making it hard to sleep at night and giving her headaches.

In order to avoid comparisons to NerveGear and its *SAO* Incident, and to ensure such a horrible thing could never happen again, the AmuSphere had been designed with an almost excessive number of safeguards. It constantly monitored the senses and automatically shut down if the body's condition started to worsen, forcing the player back into reality.

The last thing she wanted was for that to happen during the tournament, so Karen paid close attention to her physical condition. She had to beat Pitohui in SJ2. It was a game, but not something she was playing. Two lives hung in the balance.

So she stayed in the world of *GGO* as long as time and health allowed. Eventually, her older sister complained, "You never answer the phone when I call you anymore. What's going on? You're still home, right? Are you concentrating that hard on your reading? Or...Karen, are you getting depressed because you haven't made any friends? With that and the sudden haircut—did something happen? If you've got problems and you don't want our parents to know, you can still tell me."

It was very hard for Karen to throw her off the trail.

Miyu, on the other hand, was the polar opposite. She was a completely compulsive addict—er, a "very dedicated VRMMO gamer."

There was no point at which Llenn dived into *GGO* and Fukaziroh wasn't already there. When Llenn landed in SBC Glocken, Fukaziroh would get a notification from the game that a member of her squadron was present, and she'd immediately send a message so they could rendezvous.

When they met up, Fukaziroh would always flash a toothy smile and a thumbs-up.

"All righty! Let's go hunt some monsters! Or kill some people—whatever!"

They'd go out into the wilderness to fight, in difficult zones that weren't for new players like Fukaziroh at all, but as Llenn expected, it was no trouble for her. Fukaziroh didn't act recklessly; she perfectly understood Llenn's role as the up-close combatant, and she learned the monsters' attack patterns quickly, firing her powerful grenades from a distance with great accuracy.

I can't get left behind! Llenn gathered her resolve. In order to test herself, she took greater risks than she ever did before. She tried out maneuvers she'd never attempted, and if she fell on her head, it wasn't a problem. The point was to keep moving, moving, moving: shoot, change magazines, shoot, practice.

Speed is my armor! Rushing closer is my defense!

Don't stop! Stopping means death! Just keep shooting!

P-chan II crackled pleasantly with gunfire, speaking Llenn's fiery motivations for her.

Llenn's only goal was to beat Pitohui.

She would kill her...

...to save her.

Llenn and Fukaziroh trained like the hot-blooded protagonists of shonen manga, but they weren't the only ones practicing.

"One more time! Rosa, shoot longer and keep the target in place! Anna, reload that gun faster! Your aim is fantastic, so be confident in yourself! Tanya and I will find a way to match the timing of our charge better! Don't blindly trust the bullet circle when you fire! You're wasting time waiting for the circle to appear! If you think you have the shot, take it! We can do this!"

Other players were just as busy attempting to improve their game. This, of course, was Saki—aka Eva, the boss—and her gymnastics team. They'd finished their high school finals, and more and more of their school schedule was half days now.

They were spending at least two hours in the game each day, and often more. They had team practice, too, of course, but they spent it in the game world, using the excuse, "We need this to improve our sense of unity."

In *GGO*, there were no ammo rations. You had to scavenge or buy your own. Aside from hunting monsters, where you earned experience, items, and credits, just performing simple firing practice cost you money for all that ammo. But they went ahead and practiced with their live-ammo guns anyway.

Earning experience and skill proficiency was an important part of character progression, but as athletes themselves, they keenly understood that they also needed to improve their own skill as players—boosting reaction speed and making quick decisions.

The snipers Anna and Tohma homed in on targets hundreds of yards away and shot them down, all to improve their accurate range. Quickly dispatching sudden foes that popped up nearby was part of the training, too.

A sniper's job wasn't just to take out distant targets. Performing one-hit kills at medium range in ways that other soldiers couldn't do was part of the role.

Tanya and her Bizon SMG, on the other hand, operated on sheer agility, like Llenn. In a mazelike zone full of cover, she sped around without slowing, practicing a quick trigger finger to gun down enemies the moment they appeared—even if she ran into obstacles in the process.

When that was done, an even harder regimen began. In a wide-open area, they had Tanya run around with a six-foot rope and a banner tied to her back. From a distance, her teammates then tried to shoot the banner. This practice was meant to help them hit high-speed characters like Llenn. If they actually hit Tanya, it would do considerable damage. They had to focus.

Boss and Tanya also had separate practice with the Strizh 9 mm pistol. First, they had the other four stand still and hold up wooden targets about the size of a human head.

"Ready...fire!"

Then, from firing position with their Vintorez and Bizon, they tossed the main guns away and quick-drew their pistols. This was in case their main weapons were damaged or they ran out of ammo. If they missed, they would hit their friends in the face with a 9 mm bullet.

Another group of players spotted this madness out in the open. They watched through binoculars for a little while.

"Those women are scary... They don't seem to have noticed us. Let's keep it that way."

"Got it. No use in getting hurt right at the end of a good hunt."

"They're all huge, burly chicks, too... I bet they're all, like, old ladies who have been playing online for thirty years..."

They demurely passed on their chance for an ambush.

*   *   *

Time in *GGO* was linked to real time, and the sun was setting.

They'd finished up with their risky training, and now it was time to return to the real world.

"I have something to say, girls. It's important," said Boss.

It wasn't an order, but the others formed a line at attention and waited anyway.

"We've gotten a lot tougher. If we make the most of our training in SJ2, I think we've got more than a passing shot at winning. But…"

Boss's expression hardened further. She had a powerful enough face as it was. If a little child saw her now, they would burst into tears.

"We have powerful rivals. Remember the large man working with Llenn last time, named M. I don't have confirmation, but I'm certain he'll be competing again. He's an incredible sniper, and based on what the video showed, he's got a powerful shield, too."

The other members nodded in understanding.

M's shield was like a folding screen fashioned out of spaceship armor plates, and it was powerful enough to deflect a 7.62 mm round at close range—the strongest caliber bullet they used.

If he used that out in the open and pulled off a sniping string with his M14 EBR, he could easily wipe them all out by himself. Part of the reason for that was that M could somehow snipe without creating a bullet line, even when they knew his location.

He wasn't actually cheating; he was just shooting by not touching the trigger until he was ready to pull. That didn't bring up the bullet circle that was meant to help him—meaning he was aiming strictly through the scope of the rifle and judging where to fire on his own.

When sniping, the farther the target, the higher the bullet needed to be aimed to account for gravity, plus wind. Add in a moving target, and there was even more mental calculation involved. It was a skill that required great precision and experience, and without the bullet circle, it was a technique that very few could actually pull off.

But M would do just that, thanks to his experience shooting actual guns overseas and his considerable time playing *GGO*.

If they wanted to win, they had to find a way to beat an enemy who shot unavoidable bullets at them from a perfect defensive position. The M14 EBR's effective range was about eight hundred yards. That was much farther than even a grenade launcher could reach.

"We need a way to break down that shield from the front! We need stronger weapons! So I propose..."

Propose what? Boss's teammates waited with bated breath for her proclamation.

"...that we go and find one tomorrow!"

✳   ✳   ✳

March of 2026 passed by without incident.

As the deadline approached, more and more teams announced their intention to participate in SJ2. Once there were more than thirty slots full on the list, a preliminary round would have to happen on the day before the final.

There were two team names at the top of the list.

SHINC, the runners-up of the last Squad Jam, Saki's gymnastics team.

MMTM, the third-place team. These were the men with the skull logo.

While all the other teams on the list were written in a white font, these two teams were listed in gold. That made it clear that they were seeded to have a bye.

Then, around noon on Wednesday, March 25th, with a full thirty teams already on the list, one new name was added.

This team, LF, which should have been the thirty-first in line, appeared in dazzling gold and shot up to number one.

*   *   *

Four minutes after that, a phone went off somewhere in Tokyo.

"What is it, Goushi? I'm just about to have a meeting with the other company president. Make it quick."

"I'll be brief, then. The team in question entered the event. Just now."

"…"

"Boss?"

"Thanks for the report. I'm looking forward to it."

"Yes, Boss. But…"

"I know. I've got events on the schedule after April fourth. Bye."

Forty minutes after that, on a dark and narrow canyon path in *GGO*, five men examined their in-game menus.

"Hey, check this out! She's in, she's in! It's the pink shrimp!"

"Which one? Ooh, you're right… The one who dodged all our shots!"

"She finally signed up. Looks like the super-snipers who whacked us from behind haven't entered yet, though."

"Maybe they won't. They seemed pretty pro to me, based on the video. Their movements, the hand signs—some people say they're base security for the ASDF. Maybe they entered for fun and got chewed out by the SO?"

"I don't care what! I don't care who! Whoever runs across Team Zen-Nippon (All-Japan) Machine-Gun Lovers is gonna go down!"

The other five members grunted in approval, hoisting their machine guns. Three seconds later, a panther-like monster that snuck up on them while they were distracted wiped out the group.

One hour after that…

"Boss! Karen—I mean, Llenn—entered the event!"

"Say what?!"

A party of six erupted into conversation at the entrance to a dungeon.

"You're right... Well...this is certainly shaping up to be fun!"

"I wonder what changed Karen's mind...?"

"No idea! And a real stoic warrior wouldn't ask! We're not going to reach out to her, even in real life! Until this thing is all over...we're enemies!"

"Roger that!"

"Once it's over, we can have a nice long chat with her and all her snacks."

"I want marshmallows. And snacks from Hokkaido."

"Her tea was really good! I bet those leaves were expensive!"

"Enough of that, ladies! No more talking! We're gonna tackle this dungeon now! And get farther than yesterday! Follow my lead!" Boss commanded.

"Raaah!" the other five bellowed. They headed down the tunnel into the underground.

*   *   *

Midday, April 1st.

The deadline for the second Squad Jam had just passed.

A rush of new entries flooded in just before the cutoff, making forty-nine in total. Three of the teams were seeded.

Partially, this rush was due to the unveiling of the grand prize on the twenty-eighth. It was rather more fabulous than expected.

The winning team would get a set of twenty assault rifles. The runner-up, ten submachine guns. Third place, ten pistols. All these prizes would come with hundreds of rounds of ammo and spare cartridges.

You could use the prizes or sell them for a considerable profit. Unlike the author from last time, this sponsor was apparently quite rich. After all, the grand prize of the previous event was simply a signed set of twenty of the sponsor's novels—a rather bitter reward.

It wasn't at all like the BoB, where a winner was sent a catalog of prizes to choose from. Karen simply had to respond to the message demanding her address. Eventually, a heavy box landed on her doorstep.

Congrats on winning! You were awesome out there! said the card in the box, which also held twenty different books about shoot-outs that she would probably never read.

"What should I do with them...?" she wondered. It didn't seem right to sell them to a used bookstore, so she still had them.

In SJ2, which no longer featured disappointing prizes, the forty-six unseeded teams would have to be narrowed down to twenty-seven for the final event. To do that, a preliminary round would occur starting at eight PM on the day before, April 3rd. The rules were sent by in-game message.

Teams would be matched up at random for the contest. It would be a single-round competition with a time limit of twenty minutes. Since the timing might conflict with contestants' work or other limitations, teams needed only a minimum of two of their members to compete.

In order to ensure that teams would make contact quickly and be unable to escape, the battle arena was a special rectangular one measuring one kilometer by three hundred meters, on flat ground, with many barricades strewn about. All matches would happen simultaneously under the same conditions.

To win, obviously, you had to wipe out the other team, no matter how many members. If time ran out, the side with fewer casualties won.

If that number was the same, the side that took less damage won.

If that was the same (for example, if no one suffered any damage), the side that shot fewer bullets won.

If even that was the same (for example, if neither side shot even once, and both simply ran away the whole time), it would be decided by coin flip.

The winner of every match, naturally, earned a trip to the final. That would fill in twenty-three of the teams but still left a loser's bracket of four slots. This would be filled by the losing teams with the least number of deaths, followed by those that survived for the longest time, then those with the least damage, then those that fired the fewest shots. And any team that lost a coin toss would not be eligible for a loser's slot.

None of the preliminary rounds would be aired to the public. There was no way for teams to know which other teams would move on to the main event, unless they happened to be one of the four losing teams brought back.

Fukaziroh and Llenn sat in a restaurant within *GGO*, perusing the rules.

"Wow, it's so much easier for us," noted Fukaziroh.

"I'm really glad we have a bye. There are times when only having two members helps in Squad Jam, but it's terrible for a one-on-one preliminary battle."

Like it or not, the second Squad Jam was in just three days. They were in a restaurant, rather than out in the open, and in a private room, too, to ensure that nobody else overheard them while they went over the rules.

She could have just done this over a video call with Miyu, who was up in Hokkaido, but doing it this way suited the mood better.

"Did you read the rules?"

"I did. But you wanted to go over them, right, Llenn?"

Miyu could be something of a goofball, so Llenn wanted to be certain they were on the same page. She nodded earnestly.

"Well, it's good to be thorough," Fukaziroh agreed, calling up her window to order drinks. She got her favorite carbonated lemonade, which she always drank in *GGO*, and Llenn's preferred iced tea.

The drinks jumped up out of a hole in the middle of the table. So did some fried snacks and beef jerky. Llenn's face crinkled into a smile.

"You do love your snacks, Llenn. Eat up."

"I guess I do. And eat up I shall. Thanks! Now…"

They went back over the rules, occasionally popping treats or straws into their mouths.

For the most part, it was the same as last time. Thirty teams of six members max fought it out in a battle royale taking place on a square map that was exactly ten kilometers to a side. All other teams were enemies, although anyone could fight together if they wanted.

"And we won't know the map until we get there, right?" Fukaziroh asked.

Llenn nodded.

The terrain of the special event map would be unrealistically varied, she suspected. There would be a cramped city, a thick forest, and a wide-open desert. And the starting locations were determined at random, so they would have to be prepared to fight anywhere.

"I wear subdued colors, but you go with pink, right? Don't you stick out whenever you're not in the wasteland or desert?"

"Yeah, that's why I have a camo poncho. I learned that in the last one."

Previously, she'd started in the disadvantageous forest and had to hide herself using M's camo poncho. Without that, the team of machine gunners might have spotted her even before they saw her on the scanner.

So Llenn got another green camo poncho and threw in a plain white one in case of snowfields, too. She also had some for Fukaziroh.

"Ooh, you're so prepared! Thanks."

At the time of the game's start, each team was guaranteed to be placed at least a kilometer away from any other team. From there, they could move, look for enemies, and attack.

However, there was also a feature called the Satellite Scan designed to prevent teams from simply hiding the whole time. This system provided locational data on all teams at intervals of ten minutes, when a satellite flew overhead.

"You'll get something called a Satellite Scan terminal just before the start of the event. It'll show you the map on a smartphone-type screen, and it can also project a 3-D version of it."

While the scan was happening, it displayed the location of each team leader. If the team was still alive, the dot would be bright white. If the team had been wiped out, it would be dark gray.

"I see—so you can only hide in the same spot for up to ten minutes. And because it only shows the team leader, you can set lures, the way that you did last time. On the other hand, when you only have a maximum of six members, it's not the best strategy to split up your strength like that. And if the team leader dies, then it transfers down the list, I assume. You'll be first, right?"

Llenn nodded in affirmation. "Now, this part is where the rules for SJ2 are different," she prefaced, zooming in on a part of the rule book.

In the first event, team names were not displayed on the map, but in this event, touching the team dot will display its name.

That was the same way the BoB worked.

"In other words, ten minutes after the start, you'll be able to know which team is where," Fukaziroh concluded.

Llenn raised an index finger. "Yes! And this change is very welcome for us! That means we can find out exactly where Pito is! She's on team PM4, so remember that one!" she said. Goushi had sent her a secret e-mail with the name of Pitohui's team in it.

This was the target they needed to attack first in SJ2. While it wasn't fair to the other teams, who would be doing their best in the spirit of the event, the girls were going to ignore them if possible. If anything, they ought to run around and avoid battle, staying out of sight until they reached their target.

"PM4, got it. I guess they picked *four* because it's the unlucky number that represents death. 'The death of Pitohui and M.' That's wild."

"I was kind of stunned when I realized that, too…"

"Or maybe it's just supposed to mean four PM. A late-afternoon snack."

"If only… Also, the team named SHINC is the one made up of the gymnastics team from my college's attached high school. They're really tough, so we'll try to avoid them—just run away at full speed. I did tell them I'd fight them next time, but…you know. Of course, if I do beat Pito, then I'll give them a real battle."

"Awww, why just them? Let's kill all the other teams! Why don't you shoot for being the consecutive champion?"

"Ha-ha-ha, I like your enthusiasm. Watch out for MMTM—they're tough, too. I see a few other teams from the last time…but they didn't even show the names on the video feed, so we won't know what they're like or what gear they use until we run across them. My point is…be wary of everyone," Llenn warned. Then her face clouded over, and she sighed.

"What's up? You need to use the bathroom? Can you go alone? Want company?"

"No!"

In VR, there was no need for that. Fukaziroh was perfectly aware of that, of course.

"No, I'm just wondering, can I even beat Pito? I mean…if I screw up, people could die as a result…," Llenn said, on the verge of tears.

The blond apprentice witch grinned devilishly. "There's no use worrying about that now, is there? If we fail on the big day, you can worry about it then. You haven't had enough liquor—that's all."

Fukaziroh waved her left hand, and another iced tea shot up out of the middle of the table. "Drink up. It's on me."

"Thank you… Say, Fuka—I mean, Miyu. Thanks a lot."

"For what? You really love that iced tea that much?"

"No, that's not what I meant! Thanks for hanging out with me and taking time away from your favorite game to come to *GGO* and enter SJ2 with me." Llenn bowed deeply.

"Come on. Since when do women need to put their friendship into words? You're embarrassing me," Fukaziroh said brusquely. "And don't worry—I'll make sure you pay me back."

"Got it! I'll do whatever I can for you!"

"Then, I guess I might accept awesome VIP seats at an Elza Kanzaki concert."

"Ugh! The hardest request of all…"

CHAPTER 5

SECT.5

The Event Begins

CHAPTER 5
The Event Begins

Saturday, April 4th, 2026.

At just around noon, there was a noticeable uptick in the number of people from Japan diving onto the *GGO* Japanese server.

"All set... Good!"

In a high-rise apartment in warm and sunny Tokyo, Karen Kohiruimaki closed the curtains on her windows to shut out the light, changed into pale-yellow pajamas, adjusted her air conditioner and humidifier, then lay down on the bed with her AmuSphere in place.

"It's time to do this! It's time for me...to save her life!"

"Whoops, look at the time. Gotta go."

In the dining room of a house in snowy Hokkaido, Miyu hastily slurped down the last of a pack of instant yakisoba noodles and drank the rest of the soup in her cup. Lastly, she washed it all down with tea from a plastic bottle.

She then rushed to the bathroom and then her bedroom. She flopped onto her bed without bothering with pajamas.

"All right, time to kick some ass."

Then she reached out and grabbed a well-used AmuSphere.

"But before that, maybe I should have a bit of ice cream for dessert!"

Miyu let go of the AmuSphere and headed for the refrigerator.

In homes around the capital city, teenage girls put on their AmuSpheres.

All around Japan, many men and a smattering of women put on their AmuSpheres.

And in one luxury apartment in Tokyo with the curtains drawn, a young woman marveled, "Ooh, this is so exciting!"

She stood in the darkness, totally nude. At her side was a huge object, like a horizontal cocoon that was nearly nine feet long.

"And now..." She pressed something, and part of the giant cocoon opened. On the inside, lit by red LEDs, was a thick liquid more than a foot deep.

It was a device called an isolation tank or a float tank. You would float in a high-salinity fluid as warm as body temperature, and when the lights inside the tank turned off, you were in a world without sound, light, smell, touch—even gravity.

By shutting off all human senses, one was plunged into the ultimate relaxation, allowing for recuperation of tired muscles and mental processes. Naturally, this also worked wonders for going on a full dive.

Normal AmuSphere use did cut out nearly all bodily senses, but it was said that some small amount of surface noise got through. By going into an isolation tank, you could almost perfectly remove all real-world stimuli. It was no wonder that the most enthusiastic and dedicated players wanted them so badly.

Relaxation facilities and high-end online cafés offered rentals of these isolation tanks, but to buy them cost anywhere between a cheap car and a luxury vehicle, depending on the model. Only the richest players could afford to keep one in their homes.

"Now, will I come out of this alive...?" wondered the naked woman with excitement as she entered the tank.

Right next to it was another, identical tank. That one had a hook that had been amateurishly welded onto the lid—along with a heavy padlock to ensure it couldn't be opened from the inside.

Like in the previous event, the SJ2 event hall was a large bar in SBC Glocken.

The participants had gathered there by 12:40 PM to wait and were teleported to the waiting area at 12:50. They then had ten minutes to materialize and equip whatever weapons and gear they were using. At exactly 1:00, SJ2 would begin, and all members would be teleported somewhere onto the map.

Thus would begin a merciless sequence of slaughter that would abate only when one team remained. The developers would capture and broadcast video of the battle. Special markers that represented cameras flew around the area, capturing the most dynamic as possible angles for the action.

Anyone, including any defeated participants, who wanted to watch the event live could sit in the bar, drinking and eating, watching the battle unfold, and yelling at the screen.

The first Squad Jam had taken an hour and twenty-eight minutes, but it had been among twenty-three teams without a prior round. This one had a full thirty teams involved. Whether that meant it would take longer to settle or the increased numbers would mean fiercer and shorter fighting was anyone's guess.

The bar was packed by 12:20. Participating players had shown up in small groups. They traded comments like "Good luck" and "You're not gonna beat us this time" and "We're gonna slaughter you all."

As in the last Squad Jam, there wasn't a bookie taking bets for SJ2 like there had been for the BoB. It was an administrative issue; the higher-ups couldn't spare the resources to protect against cheating the way they did for the larger event.

Instead, there was another activity; people could submit guesses for the number of total shots fired in the event—a competition that got participants very heated. The numbers submitted this time were much higher than in the first Squad Jam.

Meanwhile, there were a few teams whose arrival at the pub cast ripples of silence outward as the crowds noticed them.

One was Team MMTM, the seeded third-place squad from last time. That moniker was just an abbreviation for the official title of the squad: Memento Mori—Latin for *Remember, you must die*. The saying meant that everyone dies eventually, so it was important to lead a full life without regrets.

Six men wearing shoulder patches with the insignia of a skull holding a knife in its mouth marched into the bar. In the last event, they'd worn their own individual outfits in camo of different colors, but this time, they showed off their heightened intent by coordinating.

It was an outfit used by the Swedish military—a rather stylish green-based camouflage pattern featuring blocky patches made from straight lines that went against the norm. Like other characters, they wore camo tops and bottoms, combat boots, and no other major items. Their weapons and armor were completely shut away in their item storage—but anyone who'd watched them last round would know what they liked to use.

For their main weapons, this squad had an HK21 7.62 mm machine gun and five precision European assault rifles. That is, assuming there hadn't been any changes in the last two months.

"If I could bet on this, I'd put my money on them."

"It's a safe choice. They've got the highest total strength as a team," said some onlookers.

Six women entered after that group, and the sight of them was enough to subdue the excited buzz in the tavern all over again.

They were six Amazons of various types dressed in camo of a multitude of fine green spots: a gorilla with braids, a blond beauty wearing shades, a squat and wide dwarf, a middle-aged lady from the neighborhood, a silvery fox, and a coolheaded lady with black hair.

Despite women being a rare sight in *GGO*, no one in the bar dared to catcall them with a thoughtless *Hey ladies! Lookin' good!*

SHINC was the second-place team from the last event, and the team that had racked up the most total kills by far. Many of the people in that very bar had been killed by them.

The leader of MMTM was a handsome fellow who was a skilled player and a participant in the BoB. He slipped away from his group as they got ready to lead a toast, and he walked over to the gorilla-like woman with the figure of a pro wrestler, Boss.

"Hello, ladies. We didn't run into you last time, but I'm looking forward to the opportunity today. Don't die until that can happen, all right?" he said with an impertinent smile.

Boss smiled back at him, with more ferocity than seduction. "But of course. I do hope you gentlemen will introduce your-selves before you get killed. Otherwise, we might not even notice it's you," she taunted in a very ladylike fashion.

The entire bar roared at this—even the other members of MMTM, who slapped their table as they laughed.

The team leader wasn't a small enough man to get angry about it.

"This should be a good one! I'm glad you decided to enter!" He grinned, gave them a two-fingered wave, and returned to his group.

About two minutes after the Amazons had disappeared into their own private room at the pub, a giant of a man loomed inside the door.

"Look, it's him…"

He was a good six feet tall, with a chest as thick as a break-water, arms like pipes, the physique of a foreign bodybuilder, and wavy brown hair. He wore venomous-green camo pants that looked fit to burst around his thighs, and a brown T-shirt that per-fectly exhibited his musculature.

No one who'd seen the previous Squad Jam needed an explana-tion of who he was.

This was M.

The man who'd formed a two-person team with the pink shrimp. Though their battle scenes had been few, they'd emerged victorious from each one and triumphed over the team of Amazons in the final battle. The man who'd wielded the M14 EBR with practiced ease, along with a shield capable of deflecting 7 mm bullets.

He was also the man who'd fired his pistol at the little girl partway through and ended up getting shot instead, then worked separately from her for a bit.

The onlookers had a number of theories as to why they'd suddenly split up. Some said they'd simply had differences of opinion when it came to their next strategy. Some said their information had somehow been leaking to the Amazons through the audience, and it had been a crafty strategy to pretend they were arguing and thus trick the other team.

Ultimately, it was still a mystery, and no one had the guts to ask him about it for themselves.

At the very, very end of the battle, the man had shown up again and helped the shrimp with incredible sniping. He'd dispatched three of the Amazons and helped his squad win.

The members of MMTM, who had lost in the battle on the shoreline against M, glared at him from a distance.

"He's playing after all… The man without a bullet line…"

"This is a revenge match. If we run across him, we do like we practiced," they said.

Five of them had been taken out by M's specialty, sniping without a bullet line. No wonder they had it in for him.

Behind M entered more people, who appeared to be his teammates. There were four men, all wearing the same camo pattern. The eerie pattern, which was reminiscent of reptile skin, combined patches of green and brown in equal measure and seemed likely to come in handy in both desert and forest environments.

"What the hell is that?"

But the feature that startled the onlookers was the identical camo masks that completely covered the heads and faces of those four men, plus tinted goggles that hid their eyes. There was no way to tell who they were.

Masks and goggles are all fine and good in battle, but why do they need them now? wondered all the people present. The only way to tell the four apart was their radically varied body types.

One was short—by *GGO* standards, at least—at about five five.

One was large—not as large as M but close to six feet—and beefy.

One was slender, about five seven but with limbs like sticks.

One was tubby, with a round, extruding gut and the silhouette of a sumo wrestler.

The four followed M without a word or a glance around them. Despite the artificial nature of the sensory information in VR games, there was something of an aura in their manner that spoke volumes to every person in the pub.

"They look tough."

"Yeah…maybe they're hiding their faces because people would recognize them."

"They might even be BoB-level guys."

The crowd was convinced that the four were very tough. M was one half of the previous champion team, and now he had an eerie bunch with him. What did he have up his sleeve this time? People were eager to find out.

It was in the midst of this tension that a woman's voice called out, "Yoo-hoo! Thanks for waiting, everybody!"

All the people who'd followed M's party with their eyes turned back to the entrance, where a female character was now standing.

She was about five foot nine, with her black hair tied into a ponytail high on the back of her head. She wore a formfitting bodysuit in navy blue. Her skin was tan, and her body was slender but fully muscled, without a hint of any feminine softness or bounty to it.

Her facial features were attractive, if sharp, but the brick-red geometric tattoos she had on either cheek made her eerie, to say the least.

"Well, well, well! Sorry to keep you all waiting! You're here to see me in action, I presume! Very nice! Look forward to the show!" she chattered, showering the room with attention.

"…"

But the bar patrons just stared at her, openmouthed, unsure of how to react. She was the sixth person to enter right after the five men, so she was presumably part of their team. So why was she so much less reserved than the others?

"Heya! Hi there! Thanks for the support!" she continued. What was this, a campaign stop? She looked around and waved left and right as she made her way through the bar.

The patrons talked among themselves at volumes that suggested they didn't care whether she overheard them.

"What's that all about? Is she on M's team, too?"

"That's what I'm guessing. But she seems a bit…out of place?"

"Is she the princess the knights are there to protect?"

"Remember that term people used to say like a decade ago? The 'princess of the geek club'?"

"Never heard of it—too old. Is that like some kind of TV show?"

"No, it's what happens when there's one girl who enters a group that's otherwise solely comprised of male nerds. They all shower her with attention, so basically any girl can be a princess that way."

"Are you actually…way older than me, sir?"

"Don't get all respectful with me, dick."

"So you're saying that guy and the other four…are supposed to be the princess's guards? Does that mean they're not gonna go all out in the fight? That would be a letdown…"

"She's a pretty lady. Get rid of the facial tattoos, and she'd be right up my alley. Think she just started? Man, I'd love to give her private lessons on how to shoot…"

"You freak."

"Oh, so you're saying a hot woman like that in your presence wouldn't get you at attention? Are you some old geezer in real life?"

"Only kids ask about personal details."

"What'd you say to me?"

"Knock it off, you guys. For one thing, there's no guarantee that the player is the same age as the character..."

While the men continued their unsolicited commentary about her looks, the woman vanished into the private room where M had gone.

"It's her...Pitohui... I can't believe that bitch is still in *GGO*...," grumbled a man.

"You know her, Leader?" asked Jake, the HK21 machine gunner, surprised. The other members of MMTM looked equally confused.

It's amazing that our leader actually knows the name of a female character, they all thought. That was because, in his stoic pursuit of success in the game, he intentionally ignored anything feminine. The Amazons were a very noticeable exception.

With a truly displeased look, their leader answered, "Over a year ago, right after *GGO* had started...we were in a squadron together for a real short time. She didn't have those tattoos then, and her hair was short to make fighting easier, and she didn't wear that outfit."

"Ohhh. I never knew that," Jake replied.

"Because I never told anyone. All the players were still new to the game, when everyone was getting by with dinky guns and trying to get better. Those were good times..."

"Stop reminiscing, Leader."

"But why didn't you keep playing with her? Was she too weak?"

The leader shook his head and downed his (nonalcoholic) drink. "She was really tough. For one thing, she moved so naturally. I don't know for sure, but I have a hunch that she was really familiar with full-diving already."

"So why didn't you stay friends?"

"I couldn't."

"Why not?"

"She doesn't think of comrades as friends. If she's about to die, she'll use her companions as a shield. If you're standing next to a monster, she'll happily throw a grenade your way. If her party member dies, she'll still be smiling. Even if *she* dies. You can't play with someone who just wants to die. I live by the saying 'Remember you must die.' But she lives by the saying 'I wish I could forget I'm alive.'"

"She sounds crazy... No wonder you wanted out."

"From what I hear, after she quit my squadron, she did the same thing with the next one. Eventually, no one would group with her, so she stopped trying. The name Pitohui's a taboo among all the old-school players who are in the know."

The other MMTM members reacted with shock, disgust, and shrugged shoulders.

"Why's she teaming up with M for this, then?" one of them asked.

"No idea... I couldn't say—but be careful. I'll get my revenge, obviously, but don't get careless out there. We have no idea what these guys are gonna do," the leader said, dead serious.

The others nodded.

He paused before adding, "Do any of you know where the name Pitohui comes from?"

"I couldn't imagine."

"No idea."

"Same."

"It sounds cute."

"Is it some fairy?"

After the five answered, the leader explained, "It's the name of a bird. A bird that only lives in New Guinea, I think."

"Oh. That's cute," Jake blurted out. The leader's eyes narrowed.

"Cute? You think that's cute? Pitohuis have a neurotoxin

powerful enough to kill any human that touches them. It's the perfect name for her."

The table fell silent.

"Don't get careless," he repeated.

Most of the groups of five and six that entered the bar were SJ2 participants who did not attract nearly the same kind of attention. The crowd just ignored them.

It wasn't hard to imagine all those teams thinking, *Heh, you'll be looking at us differently when this is all over! I'll be the next hero/heroine of the game.*

Among those groups was one of four men and a single woman. The difference between the smiling men and the extremely disgruntled, silent woman was jarring.

Her avatar age appeared to be late twenties, and her features themselves were simple and attractive. The color of her neat, bobbed hair was the brilliant green of young leaves. It was a color you rarely saw in real life, but it didn't seem out of place in *GGO*'s sci-fi setting at all. There were plenty of anime-style hair colors here.

Her outfit matched those of the four men, with brown cargo pants and high-top boots. On top, she wore just a simple black T-shirt. It was hard not to notice her impressive bust.

While her appearance may have drawn the interest of a number of male players, the look on her face successfully kept any of them from talking to her.

Time continued to pass, until the start of the second Squad Jam had nearly arrived.

The men (and the few women) participating in the event began wrapping up their virtual meals and drinks. A crackling tension filled the air.

As the urge to fight pulsed throughout the bar, one question began to coalesce, and a few souls began to wonder about it aloud.

They said, "Still no sign of her? Is she not playing?"

"You mean the pink shrimp who won last time?"

It was now 12:45. If she didn't enter the bar in the next five minutes, she'd be disqualified from participating for being late.

"Still not here yet...?" murmured Tanya, the one with very short silver hair, as she peeked through the private-booth curtain.

"Center yourself," murmured Rosa, the gruff mother at her side.

"..."

Boss's severe face was motionless, as silent as a boulder.

Two minutes passed, then three.

At 12:48, it seemed as though she really was going to be late. The previous champion of the event was actually going to get disqualified.

"We made it!"

"Whew! That was a close one!"

The final two players yelped as they rushed into the building.

They both wore brown robes that hid their faces and bodies, but their heights and voices made it obvious they were female. No one would mistake a figure that short. It was Llenn the champion, she of unnatural speed and strategy.

The other person with her was similarly tiny and female. She would seem to be Llenn's partner this time. The bar broke into murmurs and cheers now that everyone realized the champ had avoided a very embarrassing disqualification.

"She's here! It's Llenn, the champion!"

"In another two-person team? Talk about confident..."

"I guess she figures better two elite players than six useless lumps?"

"I'm hopin' for more slaughter than last time!"

"That other one under the robe looks like a girl, too. I can tell by the smell."

"Oh, I see. So you're a sicko."

And so on, went the men in attendance. For their part, Llenn and Fukaziroh seemed utterly unperturbed by the attention they were attracting.

"Do we have time for a drink, Llenn?"

"You want *more*? You're not going to get thirsty here! Why do you care?"

"For the atmosphere. C'mon, let's have a toast! To our impending victory!"

"For atmos… Ugh, are you going to get a stomachache again?"

"Listen, I'll be fine! I've already expelled anything that might upset it!"

In fact, Llenn and Fukaziroh should have been there twenty minutes ago. They were going to meet up in town, nice and simple, before Llenn took her friend to the event location.

But as soon as they'd started walking together, the safety function of Fukaziroh's AmuSphere had kicked in and forcibly shut it down. Llenn's friend had simply vanished before her eyes. After several minutes without her return, Llenn had sent a panicked message to Fukaziroh and gotten a response from Miyu's smartphone.

OH CRAP. I ATE THAT ICE CREAM TOO FAST, AND MY STOMACH'S RUMBLING UP A STORM.

"Whaaaaat?" Llenn had shouted, so stunned that she'd been afraid her AmuSphere would shut down, too. A few minutes later, she'd texted again.

DONE YET?

IT'S STILL RUMBLING.

STIIIILL?

I'M WIPING MY BUTT NOW. CRAP, I RAN OUTTA PAPER!

JUST HURRY UUUUP!!

At last, they'd met up again and sprinted to the bar, just barely making it inside in time.

"Phew…"

Llenn already felt like she'd just been through a battle. She didn't have the willpower to go into a private room, so she settled down on a sofa by an empty table near the door.

Fukaziroh joined her and promptly ordered the usual sparkling lemonade and iced tea. They appeared in the center of the table. There was less than a minute before the event started.

Llenn stared up at the ceiling in exhaustion and heard a familiar voice say, "Hey! Llenn!"

"…"

She looked over at the source of the voice. After how long it'd been since they'd last seen each other, Pitohui was still very much Pitohui. It was both comforting and terrifying.

"Congrats on winning the last round!" Pitohui said with a very familiar, dazzling smile.

"Thanks!" Llenn replied, forgetting everything else for just a moment.

The next moment, a voice-over announced that in thirty seconds, all SJ2 participants would be teleported to the waiting area.

"Whoops, guess we don't have time to sit around and chat," Pitohui said sadly, the tattooed skin around her eyes stretching.

"Pito," Llenn started, standing up with her iced tea in hand.

"Hmm?"

"I'm going to do my best, and I hope you look forward to that. Please…don't forget your promise."

Pitohui blinked. "Huh? I don't know what you mean…but okay. And enough of the formal stuff! Anything else to get off your chest in the last few seconds?"

Llenn's answer was instantaneous. "You'll die by my hand."

"Ha-ha!" Pitohui laughed joyfully and walked away.

Llenn sucked down a huge gulp of tea through her straw, then looked down at Fukaziroh, who was still seated. "Let's go, partner."

"You got it!"

Then the teleportation began.

Llenn scowled. But Fukaziroh was rushing to slip her straw into her mouth. "H-hang on—I wanna get one last—"

They vanished in a spray of light.

In the ten minutes they spent in the dark waiting area, every character materialized their weapons and gear for battle.

Llenn showed Fukaziroh how the Satellite Scan terminal worked, and the other girl picked it up immediately. This smartphone-like object was the lifeline of Squad Jam. Players couldn't destroy it, but they could lose it, so they had to be very careful not to drop it.

As Llenn had suspected, there was an announcement that made it clear the scanner would no longer be an indestructible object. It would exist in physical space, but any attack (including bullets, of course) would pass right through it.

In the empty black space before them was a large readout that said TIME REMAINING: 04:33, ticking down each second. Llenn was now in pink warrior mode, every piece of gear equipped, with nothing left to do but wait.

Her outfit was exactly the same as last time. Her clothes were—from toes to fingers to the top of her cap—totally pink. She also wore a pink bandana around her neck.

P-chan II, her trusty P90, hung from a sling strap over her shoulder. There were six backup magazines in pouches on either thigh for easy access. Any more might impede her mobility, so she went with what was familiar.

But this time, she had nine more in her inventory, three times as many as before. The P90 could shoot fifty bullets from a mag, so with sixteen mags in total, that made eight hundred bullets.

She also had an extra optional part for the P90 this time, but it was still in her inventory for now.

As far as thrown weapons went, she was bold this time: not a single plasma grenade. She didn't want them to get hit by a bullet and explode while they were hanging off her belt, and the weight difference would allow her to pack a few more extra magazines.

For her truly final resort, she had a black combat knife, twelve inches long and mean, attached behind her lower back so she could reach around and pull it out backhand with her right hand.

The only health-restoring items you were allowed to use in SJ2 were the emergency medical kits that every player was automatically given in their item storage. One healed 30 percent of a player's full HP, but the effect happened over a span of 180 seconds, making it relatively useless in the midst of battle.

Still, Llenn had made use of all three of hers in the prior Squad Jam. Without them, she would've died. So she had them in an easy-to-reach pouch on her body, hoping she wouldn't need them.

She wanted to keep her on-person belongings as minimal and light as possible, but the monocular with the distance gauge was a must, so she had that in a pouch behind her back. Like the knife, this was something she had borrowed from M last time around. With the credits she'd earned during her training ramp-up, she'd bought her own to use. She didn't know what the circumstances would be when she needed to use it, so it wasn't dyed pink.

And the multiple ponchos in different colors for different terrain? She wouldn't forget those in her storage; they were light enough to carry.

"Can't we start yet?" wondered Fukaziroh, who, like Llenn, was all decked out for slaughter. She wore a big helmet over her tied-up blond hair. On her torso were the MultiCam-pattern jacket and the green vest with bulletproof plating.

Over each shoulder was one of her MGL-140s. She'd named them Rightony and Leftania, respectively. The straps attached to the left side of the right-hand gun, as well as on the opposite side of the left-hand gun, but the positions of the guns could easily be switched with fasteners.

"They look exactly the same," Llenn had once pointed out. "If you take them off their slings, how will you know which one's Leftania and which one's Rightony?"

"That's easy! Whichever one's in my right hand is Rightony," Fukaziroh replied. Apparently, it didn't matter.

Her backpack was completely stuffed with grenades. There was a partition inside so that she could grab one each from the right and left side if she reached behind her back. Her inventory was so stuffed with grenades that she'd met the weight limit.

An M&P pistol was holstered on her right leg. There were three spare clips, making four in total with seventeen rounds each. She'd also brought her med kits, of course.

Fukaziroh asked, "What sort of stuff do you suppose other people will be packing?"

"I don't know. I bet M will have the same gun and shield, though."

"What about Pito?"

"I have absolutely no idea. She used a different gun every time I played with her. But she's strong, so I bet she can equip a lot of heavy guns. We'll have to assume she's packing serious firepower."

"And the other four?"

"I've got nothing on them…"

Belatedly, Llenn began to worry about her plan.

It was just an in-game event that was about to start, but for Pito-hui and M, it was a battle of life and death. As someone whose life wasn't in danger, could she actually stop them? Would their passion for the event outdo her own?

Llenn's expression grew clouded. Fukaziroh smacked her on the back.

"There, there. It's possible that Pito's team will win the whole thing, right? If they don't die in the game, then they won't die, right?"

"True, but…"

She couldn't just sit back and hope that it would work itself out. The most surefire way to save Pitohui's life was for Llenn to kill her, herself. That was why she was here.

Of course, if she and Pitohui were left in the final two teams, she was willing to resign in order to achieve that aim, but it seemed like beating her was the more sporting thing to do.

"Argh!"

Llenn slapped her cheeks.

Stop worrying!

Just fight!

And...kill!

Less than a minute remained now, the seconds counting down—forty-three, forty-two, forty-one, forty, thirty-nine—mercilessly fast.

Llenn pulled the loading handle of the P90 with a dry clank and loaded the first bullet into the chamber.

CHAPTER 6
Booby Trap

SECT.6

CHAPTER 6
Booby Trap

Right at one PM, the bright light receded, and their vision returned.

"This looks like...a town..."

Llenn was standing in a city street. She promptly looked around. Fukaziroh was there, six feet away, also scanning the area.

All other teams were guaranteed to be at least one kilometer away, according to the rules, so there was no worry about imminent combat. But a powerful sniper rifle with .338 Lapua Magnum rounds or a 12.7 mm antimateriel rifle could easily shoot from that distance. If they had been in a clearing, they might have had to get down and crawl immediately from the beginning.

But here, they were surrounded by houses.

"We're safe for now!" Llenn told Fukaziroh.

"Got it."

Thanks to a handy communication item that adjusted volume on the fly, whether you whispered or shouted, your voice would enter your squadmates' ears at a reasonable volume, neither too soft nor too loud. Even more impressive was the fact that the item had no distance limit, and it worked perfectly no matter where you went during Squad Jam—even inside or underground.

Once they'd confirmed they were safe, the next step was to check their location.

Llenn was standing in a foreign town.

Most of the buildings were one story, with the occasional two. It was a whole lot of plain, low-budget housing of an unfamiliar style, lined up in rows. She'd seen neighborhoods like this one in Hollywood movies before.

Along the main road was a line of storefronts, which were all shuttered up now. The streets connecting to the main road only featured houses.

The yards for the houses weren't very big. They seemed crammed together. Given that the entire setting of the game was "postapocalyptic Earth," it was a completely empty ghost town. The roofs and walls of the buildings were damaged, and many windows were broken. A number of power-line poles were tilted, the lines hanging low. The pavement was in terrible shape, often cracked and giving way to bursts of grass.

The sky overhead was clouded over. It was an eerie sight, dull gray with a little bit of *GGO*'s unique red tint to it.

Llenn's pink color was most advantageous on clear days, when the off-kilter red atmosphere made the sun as red as during sunset.

"Hmm…"

The camo effect wasn't going to be so useful this way. She might not be able to pull off any ambushes. Plus, the wind was blowing this time. On the ground, she felt a light breeze on her cheek with the occasional gust, but the clouds above were moving fast. It seemed to Llenn that they could've made the weather nice for the big event.

Temperature in VR games was calibrated such that it was always reasonably comfortable, no matter how you dressed. So there wasn't any chill against the skin, but based on the sky and the dried-out plants, it appeared the season was set to winter on this map. In fact, it looked like it might snow.

"Llenn, come check this out!" Fukaziroh called.

She joined her on the side of the house and saw something odd. "Oh? Whoa…"

It was a wall.

Between the roofs of the houses, they could see, looming several hundred yards away, a great fortress wall rising up high. It seemed about the height of a twenty-story building: say, two hundred feet tall. It was impossible to tell from here exactly how tall it was.

The wall was a plain gray color, presumably built with concrete. The skyscrapers in Tokyo were much taller, but the way it stretched from one side of the horizon to the other was intensely, uniquely oppressing.

"It's like a dam," Llenn observed.

"Oh, I see. So there's water on the other side. Guess we'll drown if it breaks," said Fukaziroh.

Llenn imagined the deluge that would sweep over them. "Fuka…just don't shoot any grenades at it."

"Okay. But I could also bust that thing with a single punch."

The wall went directly straight, then turned ninety degrees and continued at a right angle until it vanished into the distance. It probably continued a long, long way. Additionally, the wall's surface was intriguing. On the left side of the angle, there was a subtle vertically lined pattern on the concrete, and on the right side, the lines were horizontal.

"Oh…that must be the boundary of the map," Llenn said as she realized it. Both the BoB and SJ were set on special maps exactly ten kilometers to a side. Therefore, the designers had to come up with ways to define those boundaries naturally.

The third Bullet of Bullets, for example, had been set on an island. The previous Squad Jam had been surrounded by mountains and mysterious valleys to block players from leaving.

"Ah, I see. It's like they're saying 'Nobody's gettin' past *this*!' And people can't fly in this game," said Fukaziroh.

"I'm guessing these walls surround the whole thing in a square. This is just one of the corners."

"So…we're exactly in the corner of the map, then. But where, I wonder?"

All the maps of *GGO* so far had been based in the Northern Hemisphere, so this was probably no different. They knew it was one PM, so if they could see the sun, they could gauge directions, but the heavy clouds overhead prevented that.

So was the intersection of the wall up there the northeast corner? Southeast? Or the other end?

"We'll be able to figure that out soon."

Llenn retrieved the Satellite Scanner from her chest pocket and pressed one of the two switches on it. Instantly, a three-dimensional map popped into being between them, displaying terrain and buildings.

It turned out that this map was indeed surrounded by square walls.

If the map was aligned so that north was up, the leftmost quarter or so of the map was all residential. It was a long, narrow stretch of town going from north to south. The roads, large and small, proceeded in the four cardinal directions in orderly fashion, splitting the blocks into a grid pattern. It was just like Karen's hometown.

In the middle of the town was a railway going north to south. There were two open-air platforms making a small station just a bit north of the map's center.

Outside of the station was a largish rotary, but there were no tall buildings. Virtually all of them were ground-level structures. It was quite different from the last map's city, where the ruins of high-rises jutted into the sky like the teeth of a giant comb. Apparently, this place wasn't nearly as prosperous.

"*GGO* has vehicles, right? Think we can get the choo choo train running?" Fukaziroh asked, although it was hard to tell if she was only joking.

There had been trucks and hovercrafts in the last Squad Jam, so it was certainly possible there would be more rides out there. Llenn had no idea how to operate a rail vehicle, though. And if it was possible…

"Where would we go?"

"To a bigger town…to shop for clothes…?"

"After we kill Pito, maybe."

On the map, right near the northwest corner, there was a single shining dot. For just the first minute of the game, that was the indicator of their own location. Otherwise, Squad Jam was unhelpful in that it didn't display your own location except during the Satellite Scan. It was a disadvantageous system for those without a good sense of direction.

"So we're here now. In other words…right at the northwest edge of the map," Llenn said, sticking her hand into the projection to indicate the spot.

Fukaziroh nodded. "Ah, I see. Meaning…the vertical-striped wall is to the west, and the horizontal-striped wall is the one to the north."

"Yep. Vertical is west! Got it! And there are no enemies to the north or west of us right now!"

"Okay, cool! The bad guys are to the south and east! Now which way are we goin'?"

"Hang on, hang on."

They hadn't finished examining the map. Llenn ignored the overly enthusiastic Fukaziroh and resumed poring over the terrain. After all, when the fighting got fierce, they might not actually have time to examine the map during the scan. She needed to know the lay of the land first.

The northern middle of the map was rolling hills. Like her home in Hokkaido, it was a wide expanse with gentle slopes. There were no tree graphics there, so it was probably just covered in grass. It seemed perfect for sheep.

And very good for visibility, too. At the top of a hill, you'd probably be able to see the valleys and downward slopes—and vice versa. A good place to spot enemies and to be spotted in return.

"Now that's a place to watch out for snipers… We ought to avoid it if we can."

"Gotcha. They can hit you from hundreds of feet away, right? Nasty stuff."

In both the real world and *GGO*, nobody was more hated than snipers. They were angels of death, waiting around from distances that normal soldiers or players couldn't shoot from and unleashing instantaneous death. And if you didn't know where they were, you didn't even see the bullet line first.

Tohma, the Dragunov-wielding crack sniper of Team SHINC, had sniped at Llenn the last time around. The fear of that experience was still fresh in her bones.

And M was an even better sniper than Tohma. *Please don't let Pito's team be there, please don't let Pito's team be there*, Llenn prayed.

Then they looked south of the rolling hills on the map.

"What is this? Can you tell, Llenn?"

"I dunno…"

It was a rounded, dome-like structure.

"A stadium, maybe?"

"Sure looks like a stadium."

So they were in agreement on that. The appearance of it was similar to the domed baseball stadium in Hokkaido, but…

"Is a baseball stadium really that big?" Llenn wondered.

Indeed, it was much too large for that. Going by the map markings, the circle in the middle of the map was two kilometers across. And it looked like it was several hundred meters tall, too—so that was over a mile long and as much as a thousand feet tall.

"Hey, it's Earth in the future, so it might make sense. Maybe baseball gets a lot bigger," Fukaziroh suggested nonsensically. For now, they didn't really need to figure it out, so Llenn stopped worrying about it. They wouldn't know what it was until they got there. Given how much space it took up, the inside couldn't possibly be off-limits.

South of the map's center, below the dome, was a spread of green and brown. It appeared to be barren farm fields and scattered woods. It was basically flat, and while the visibility wasn't as clear as in the hills, it was a place to watch out for snipers.

Lastly, the east end of the map was depicted with mountains, both north and south. In the upper right corner, meaning northeast, the graphics suggested that the area wasn't quite so severe. Given that the color was white, it would seem to be a smooth, snowy peak. The perfect place for a ski slope, perhaps.

"I bet you could ski here. You have a pass for the lift, Llenn?"

"Sadly, I do not."

"Then we'll just have to climb…"

Fukaziroh had said it as a joke, but the more Llenn thought about it, the more likely it seemed that there could be six sets of skis hidden somewhere. Or perhaps snowmobiles.

In the southeast part of the map, to the bottom right, the slope was much steeper. This mountain was craggy and rocky, with a lot of trees—a blend of gray rock and green trees. It probably wasn't so steep that climbing was impossible, but it didn't seem easy to walk through.

A diagonally situated highway connected the mountains, running over the valley between them. The map indicated a bridge nearly two kilometers long. It was enormous, and it loomed over a hundred meters above the valley floor.

It didn't seem to be a hanging bridge, but an arch, its underside curved like a bow. A single bridge of that length without a middle support seemed totally impossible, but hey, this was future Earth—and a video game.

When the highway hit the mountain, it turned into a tunnel with no visible exit, which meant it was probably outside of the map. Surely the tunnel itself would be impossible to get all the way through. Perhaps the entrance was sealed off.

"We can cross this bridge," Llenn said, pointing at it, "but I'm going to suggest that we don't."

"Got it. They'll charge us a toll," Fukaziroh replied, deadpan.

To the east of the dome in the middle of the map, between

the mountains, there was a valley that narrowed as it went on. Within this stretch was a single, large building. There was only so much detail on the map, but the structure was clearly formidable in size.

Around it was a lot of green and blue. As for why this area was so green when the rest of the map was chilly and arid, that was another example of information the map couldn't provide.

Between those patches of greenery, there were blue patterns and lines. Blue meant water, so those would have to be little rivers, swamps, and ponds. If a river or wetland was shallow enough, you could simply run over it, but if it was deep, you'd need to put your items into your inventory and swim.

On top of that, all the water in this world setting was apparently toxic, because just being submerged in it caused a slow but continuous loss of HP. Therefore, players in *GGO* avoided going into the water as much as possible.

"I wonder what this part is...? There's plants and water, so it almost looks like a kind of maintained park... But what's this big building over here? A school, maybe?" Llenn wondered aloud.

Once Llenn was done studying the map, she looked up.

"There we go," she said.

"I can't remember all this weird and crazy terrain! In *ALO*, you just fly over everything! We didn't need maps at all!" Fukaziroh wailed.

"It's all right. I've got it all in here," reassured her partner, who had gotten lost in the residential area of the last Squad Jam and learned the necessity of understanding the terrain around you. In *GGO* and in real life, she made it a practice to look at maps and memorize them.

Thanks to that, she was now able to sprint at full speed and still know where she was going without checking her maps.

M wasn't on her team this time. She had to figure out how to fend for herself.

She'd never have learned these skills if she hadn't played *GGO* or tried out Squad Jam. And she wasn't going to hear any nonsense about women not knowing how to read maps.

"Plus, you can check the map anytime you want. Just don't lose sight of where you are at the moment. If you ever get lost and separated, stay put and call for me."

"Ugh. Roger that."

Llenn checked the wristwatch she had on the inside of her left wrist. The digital readout displayed 1:03.

Their first task would be to find a place where they could safely observe the first Satellite Scan at 1:10. There was no need to cover long distances before then. Their chances of the first team they would run into being Pitohui's were only one in twenty-nine. In fact, given M's caution, it was probably far less than that.

They'd wait for the first scan and get Pitohui's location. If they were close, great. If they were adjacent, perfect. In any case, they'd go straight for the kill.

If the team was farther off, they'd just have to find a way to get to them. They wanted to avoid enemies if possible, but getting wiped out would ruin the whole plan, so they'd have to beat anyone they could.

"All right! We're going to hide next to one of the larger houses. Follow me."

Just like the pair of girls, players all over the map looked for safe places where they could watch the first scan come in. Everyone remembered the two teams that had taken off running at the start of the last Squad Jam and wound up in the first fight.

It had happened in the northern woods, where Llenn had started. The teams had promptly engaged, wiped out half of their members, then dug in for a stubborn standoff until MMTM had ambushed them both from the side and easily knocked them out.

The golden rule of Squad Jam: "Don't do too much in the first ten minutes."

Among the other competitors, there was one man who had an idea. He called over his teammates.

"Hey! I'm just throwing this out there, but…do you think there's a way to climb that?"

He was pointing at a fortress wall with a diagonal pattern on it.

*   *   *

1:09:30.

The watches on Llenn's and Fukaziroh's wrists buzzed. That was the alarm function set to go off thirty seconds before each Satellite Scan.

They were around the side of a house facing a wide street. Llenn crouched in the shadow of a truck that had lost its wheels and rested directly on the ground, while Fukaziroh was along the wall of the house, about thirty feet away, watching the other side of the street.

If someone came traipsing down the middle of the street, they'd easily spot the two, but none of these teams were going to be that incompetent. Llenn lowered the monocular she was using to survey the area and reported, "No hostiles here."

"Nothing here, either. Boring."

"Then watch the scan on your terminal screen. Like I said, if they're close, we run away at full speed."

"Got it. And you want me to just tap all the dots and check the names? I can do that. I'm a pro at reading the alphabet."

The Satellite Scan function was modeled as though it were an actual satellite sending down data. Until it left the airspace overhead, the locations of remaining team leaders would appear as white dots on the map, and defeated or resigned teams' final locations as gray dots.

The problem was the variety of directions and altitudes that the satellites would fly in overhead, meaning the amount of time to access their data wasn't always the same.

If a particularly slow scan started from the other side of the map, that was an advantage, because they could spot their foes first—or vice versa. This was completely up to luck, so there was no way to know ahead of time how the scan would go.

They also had to touch the dots to see the names, so if the scan was quick, their fingers would have to be fast.

Llenn and Fukaziroh switched their devices on. The map appeared on the screens.

At 1:10 on the dot, the first Satellite Scan initiated.

It started directly to the north of them, the scan line moving slowly over the map from top to bottom and left to right. Perhaps the first one was intentionally slow for the players' benefit?

Here we go...

Llenn touched all the glowing dots in order, looking for the one labeled PM4.

The one in the upper left of the map was definitely theirs: LF. There were no other dots immediately nearby.

Llenn exhaled in relief. It was unlikely they'd be attacked while the scan was happening. As far as other familiar teams went, she found MMTM in the upper right—northeast. They were directly east from Llenn and Fukaziroh, on the snowy mountain near the northeast corner of the walls.

More and more dots appeared as the scan moved south, but none of them were showing PM4. She couldn't find it.

At last, all thirty dots were on the screen.

Where are they? Where, where, where?

She touched the dots, trying not to panic, then found SHINC in the southwest corner, directly south of them. Then she continued right from there, touching each and every dot...

"Got it!"

The very last one was PM4. Fukaziroh found it at about the same moment. "I got 4 PM, Llenn! At the bottom right!" she called out.

"Oh... Oh no...," Llenn mumbled. It was no wonder.

Pitohui's team was on the southeast corner of the map.

They couldn't physically be farther away from Llenn and Fukaziroh.

"Daaaaaamn iiiiiit!"

Meanwhile, as Llenn was yelling loud enough for every team on the map to hear, Pitohui sat atop one of many boulders dotting the slope and noted, "Aw, Llenn's all the way on the other side."

"..."

Over her shoulder, M stared at his screen in silence.

Meanwhile...

"Llenn's team is at the northwest edge. Over eighty percent of the map's length to the north," Boss said, feeling conflicted. The girls were on alert in a corner of the residential area.

"What shall we do?" asked Rosa, who was looking down the wide road, rather than at the scan, her PKM held at the ready.

"Sadly, it looks like it'll be a while before we fight her. Let's head to the northeast for the closest team to beat," Boss declared, instantly deciding not to worry about fighting Llenn for now.

Meanwhile...

"It's like they intentionally scattered the biggest contenders to the corners," growled the leader of MMTM, sensing the event organizers' ploy. He was on a gentle stretch of the ski-slope mountainside, using one of the few thick trees around for cover as he watched the scanner.

Behind him, running up the side of the snowy mountain like the Great Wall of China, was a gray structure with a cross pattern on it.

It was 1:11 PM.

"Why...? Aaaah!"

Was there no god in *GGO*, no merciful Buddha? Had the final war of Earth obliterated them all along with the beautiful blue sky? Or had they simply forsaken this world and packed their bags for another?

Llenn gazed up at the clouds and lamented.

"Young lady…life does not always go…the way you plan," Fukaziroh said haltingly. "And yet, you got this far…didn't you, lass? I've been watching you… Am I wrong?"

"You're right… You're right."

There's just one thing to do!

Llenn's mood pivoted suddenly. She stashed the terminal in her chest pocket, and she raced over to Fukaziroh with superhuman speed.

"We proceed southeast! Anyone who dares interfere with our lightning dash gets crushed, one at a time!"

Llenn and Fukaziroh ran through the neighborhood.

The nearest team according to the scan was about a mile south along the main road. Fortunately, the other teams had started closer to the middle of the map, so this team was the only one in the way of their mad dash.

They're obstacles! We'll wipe them out by the next scan! Then we'll zip out of the town and to the dome!

Llenn raced and raced. The paved road, cracked as it was, made the perfect surface for Llenn's fleet footwork. First, she would sprint ahead a good two hundred yards or so, then find a piece of cover and hide.

"All clear," she would relay to Fukaziroh. Then the other girl would lower her MGL-140s, hug them to her sides so they stayed put, and rush after Llenn. Once she caught up, Llenn would speed forward again.

If Llenn spotted an enemy on the way, she would not attack on the spot. There was no need. She'd duck or spin or roll behind cover—anything to avoid getting shot.

As long as she didn't get spotted, they were in control. Then she'd quietly bring Fukaziroh forward, and they'd get the jump on their foe. And even if they were spotted, as long as they didn't get hit, the situation was the same. They'd retreat, regroup, then do a coordinated attack.

The point was, not knowing where to find the enemy was a source of fear—and even more tense than the actual fighting.

The same was true for the other side, of course.

The nerves they all felt up until encountering the enemy were not at all like how it felt during a shoot-out. At least in battle players could shoot their guns at the other guys, so it even felt good, in a way.

Plus, they were located in a residential neighborhood, with plenty of features to take cover behind. Were they hiding behind that house? Aiming at them from the window there? Once players started thinking about it, they couldn't stop. It would freeze anyone in place.

C'mon! Where are you? I'm gonna find you! Llenn thought, overpowering her fear with boldness. She rushed onward, relying on her sight and quick speed to help her out.

The time passed as slowly as if she were tightrope walking over a bed of nails. Eventually, she was halfway to her original target, about eight hundred yards from the start.

"There!"

Luck was on Llenn's side.

She stopped at an intersection to check it out and, after peering around the corner, spotted the enemy team, about 150 yards off. They were in formation at a crossroads. From what she could see, there were four of them, pressed up against ruined cars and trash cans, assault rifles in hand, waiting for someone to come down the road.

With the number of teams still alive, defensive tactics like this were a smart move. Better to lie in wait for targets to come to you, rather than wander around and make yourself vulnerable.

As a matter of fact, if Llenn had been traveling down *that* road, she would've been spotted and shot at—if not actually hit.

"Found 'em. Come slowly," Llenn reported, backing away, her P90 at the ready so she could shoot as soon as she spotted anything moving.

Once Fukaziroh joined her—but still at a thirty-foot distance so they both wouldn't blow up if any of her grenades got hit—they slowly crept toward the enemy from an angle that would hide them.

The time was approaching 1:16. Llenn and Fukaziroh wanted to finish off this enemy before the next scan. Four minutes wasn't much, but gun battles often started and ended quickly, so if this plan worked, they'd have plenty of time to pull it off.

Llenn pointed at a particular house across the narrow street. "That one! You'll find the enemy camped out down the road to the left, where it meets the wider road about fifty yards down the way."

"Roger that. Ooh, it's getting exciting. All right, you ambush fairies—prepare to get blown to pieces by the grenade fairy," gloated Fukaziroh.

It didn't seem that Llenn needed to explain the plan after that point.

She snuck up from the other side of the house while Fukaziroh prepared to fire from a safer location. She'd launch her grenades on Llenn's cue. It was a maneuver they'd done plenty of times against monsters.

At this range, she wasn't likely to miss. Six grenades would explode in quick succession all around the team. In the ensuing chaos, Llenn would have an easy time picking them off with the P90, even at a slight distance.

Once they thinned out the enemy numbers—or the other guys fled—she'd charge in to finish the job. There was still the possibility that the enemy would shoot back in the desperation of their final moments. A bullet might just hit her brain stem or spine and cause instantly lethal damage.

But you'd never win a gun battle if you avoided anything that could be dangerous. Confusing recklessness with boldness would be a mistake, but the fact was, there was no winning without attacking.

"Okay, I got this."

Fukaziroh approached the house and took her firing position at the corner while Llenn waited, watching behind them. You never knew whether the enemy team was split up, or whether some other squad might approach at lightning speed.

But nothing happened.

"Almost there." Fukaziroh snuck along the side of the house and was just about to get to the perfect spot. "Hmm?"

Llenn turned back at that sound, just in time to see a hand grenade explode at Fukaziroh's feet.

There was a muffled explosion, and Fukaziroh exclaimed, "*Hweyah?!*"

Llenn saw her partner flipped backward along the wall, like someone had swept her legs out from under her.

The reason was immediately obvious: a trap.

There were fine wires strung around the corner of the house, set up to explode a small grenade if anyone tripped them. It was a very simple but effective trick that she'd used countless times against monsters.

The squad in defensive position had placed traps around the intersection, taking into account that they might be shot from the cover of nearby buildings.

"...Aaah!" Llenn groaned, realizing and cursing her mistake. She had forgotten to tell Fukaziroh something that M had warned her about.

Always watch out for grenade booby traps.

"*Hya!*"

Fukaziroh landed on her backpack. There was nothing below her shins.

The ends of her black tights were glowing with red damage effects. The force of the explosion had blown her feet right off.

In the lower left corner of Llenn's vision, she could see her team's health bars. Hers was still in full green condition, of course, but Fukaziroh's dropped until it was about three-quarters full.

Fukaziroh's toughness was impressive—she'd lost both of her feet, and that was the extent of the damage?—but Llenn couldn't sit back and relax.

"Sorryyy!" Fukaziroh wailed, but Llenn was already sprinting. She had two options.

One: Leave the immobilized Fukaziroh behind and continue SJ2 on her own at full speed.

Two: Find a way to rescue her partner, who could provide exemplary backup firepower.

Llenn chose the latter. She didn't think twice about it.

In VR games, damage conditions like losing a character's fingers or limbs were not permanent. You would return to normal in about two minutes. After all, if you were unlucky enough to lose your legs, you couldn't play the game at all after that, and what would be the point?

But the enemy squad members just fifty yards away, celebrating that they'd caught someone in their trap, weren't going to sit back and maintain their ambush state for another two minutes. At least some of them would jump out of their position and risk danger to approach—if they hadn't already.

Llenn raced over to Fukaziroh, mindful of any other traps, and pulled open the nearby front door of the house. Once she could see that there were no traps inside, she grabbed Fukaziroh's backpack with both hands.

"Yaaah!" With all her strength, she dragged her friend's body inside the house.

Fukaziroh blubbered, "I'm sorryyyy!"

Then Llenn darted back and closed the door.

In just that brief moment, she spotted the red marker that indicated one of the event's free-roaming cameras looking for battle to film was staring down at her.

The interior of the house was gloomy, as the curtains were drawn. All she could tell right away was that it had a kitchen and a living room. Llenn dragged Fukaziroh into the center of the room. The camera did not follow them inside.

A few seconds later, she heard stomping footsteps outside. There was no need to guess who it was.

Based on the intensity of the steps, it had to be at least three of them, if not more.

"I'm sorry! Leave me behind and run!" cried Fukaziroh, her stump legs splayed out in front of her.

"Only if you die," Llenn replied.

Eventually, the tense sounds of the men reached the room.

"No one's here! They're not dead!"

"Did they run away?"

Clearly, the house itself was quite cheap, given how well the sound traveled through it. But that suited Llenn just fine.

"No, that trap definitely caught 'em flush! They can't be walking around!"

She couldn't see them, but she could tell that the men were surrounding the house from a fair distance. They had their guns up, pointing straight ahead of them as they turned.

"Did they pick up their buddy and run off to the other side of the street?"

"No, I didn't see anything!"

"There wasn't time to do that!"

"Then…"

"Yeah, there's only one possibility!"

That should have been pretty obvious from the start, Llenn thought, surprisingly calm.

"They're inside this house!"

"Just run away, Llenn. I'll figure this one out," Fukaziroh pleaded quietly. That wasn't going to work. Without being able to stand and walk, the only thing she could do was shoot from the floor here.

But Fukaziroh's grenade launchers had a safety feature for the benefit of the shooter and their companions—the grenades had to travel over sixty feet before they exploded. And this house was less than thirty feet on the long side.

So what if she shot outside? She could break the glass, surely, but that was no way to aim. She *could* fight with her sidearm pistol, but it wasn't going to get her far without any mobility.

"Fuka...stay here. And stay low, as best you can," Llenn said, squeezing her P90. "I'm going to go out there and kill them."

"Whaaat?" It was too dark to see, but Fukaziroh surely had her mouth hanging open.

"I'm going to show you how a Squad Jam champion fights."

Back in the bar, the crowd was already getting very hyped. The people watching the live footage had a very clear grasp on the state of the battle.

The team with Llenn, one of the defending champions, fell right into a simple booby trap and was now trapped in a cramped little house. The camera floating over that house showed just how desperate their situation was.

It was a one-story dump. And the six men from the ambush had it totally surrounded. Four of them had 5.56 mm M16A3 assault rifles. One had an Uzi, an SMG with 9 mm pistol rounds. And one had a twelve-gauge pump-action shotgun called an Ithaca M37.

"Wait, you mean one of the big contenders is gonna lose right off the bat? Are you kidding me?!" yelled someone at the monitor. He spoke for the rest of the crowd.

The six men fanned out at ten-foot intervals around the house. Nobody was situated on the other side. You didn't want any bullets to pierce through glass or drywall and hit your teammates.

"These guys aren't stupid. They're first-timers who survived the losers' bracket, right? If they win here, that's a huge upset."

"Competition's not fair. There's only so much you can do with

just two. If they had a full six, the other four could've shot those guys up by now."

"It's all over…"

"Nah. There's no way my Llenn's gonna bow out this early, right?"

"Yeah. Wait, when did she become *yours*?"

The crowd seemed split between people feeling tense and those decidedly there to let loose. On the big monitor, the six men had their guns at the ready. They were prepared to unleash all at once.

The man with the Uzi, who seemed to be the leader, raised his left arm. The moment he dropped it, six barrels roared with gunfire, the sound erupting over the speakers of the monitor.

"Aaaah!" screamed the crowd.

They had seen, just before the hail of fire broke the house's windows, that they gave way from the *inside* first, as a pink object burst forth.

Llenn had used the length of the house as a runway, leaping at top speed and through the curtains. She held her P90 up to protect her face and dashed through the glass and torn curtains into the bright outside world. Before she hit the ground, she looked for her targets.

"There."

The first one was a man shooting an Uzi, below and to her left.

The pink object on the screen turned human in shape. It extended its right arm, and a pink object in its hand erupted in gunfire.

A number of red gunshot effects appeared on the head of the man shooting the Uzi from waist level. Five 5.7 mm bullets passed through the left side of his face and head, and he toppled to his right.

His gun continued firing as he fell, until it ran out of ammo. An icon reading DEAD flashed into the air over his body.

Next!

When her feet hit the ground, Llenn promptly tumbled forward and did three somersaults to maintain her full speed, then popped back up. Just a few feet before her was a man with an M16A3, trying to turn toward her.

He needn't have bothered.

Llenn stretched out her right arm and poured hot lead from the P90's barrel into the side of his head as he turned.

"That's two!"

The crowd in the bar was counting now.

The pink shrimp, Llenn, the defending champion, was fighting back at a speed that was just slow enough for the human eye to follow.

After she had shot the first two—more like an execution, at that range—she set her sights on the man right beyond them, using the bodies of the first two as cover.

In half a second, the man was covered in bullet holes from chest to face.

"That's three!"

The fourth target was just behind the first three casualties. He was a tall man, hastily turning the long barrel of the M16A3 in her direction.

He's close enough—I don't need to shoot, Llenn decided. She crossed the ten feet to him in a blink.

The players in the bar were surprised that Llenn held her fire.

"Huh?" "What?" "Oh?"

The pink shrimp practically teleported over to the man and slid along the ground—under his muzzle, through his legs, and to the other side.

Why didn't she shoot him? Was she going to do that now?

The crowd's questions were answered at once.

The M16A3 fell from its owner's hands. The tall man made a face like Munch's *The Scream*, except his hands were covering his crotch instead of his ears.

"Huh?" "Oof!" "Yikes!"

The camera suddenly zoomed in, and the crowd understood.

Under the man's hands, his groin was glowing bright red with the visual effect of damage. Then the camera panned down to capture Llenn, P90 in her left hand, black knife with reverse grip in her right.

At a speed faster than they could see, Llenn had drawn her knife and sliced up his groin while she passed under his legs.

"..."

All the men in the bar shivered, their eyes bulging with fear. Some even cupped their own groins in sympathetic agony.

No matter the presentation and the sensory information provided, *GGO* was still a VR game and only a simulation. Naturally, the pain it simulated was a far cry from the real thing. Getting shot left only a stinging numbness. People often compared it to the pain of acupuncture needles.

But there was no acupuncturist or shiatsu practitioner who would pierce a man's most sensitive area. Nobody could guess what the tall man on the screen was feeling at this moment. The AmuSphere had safety measures, so it wouldn't be unbearable, but it was still a new experience.

Based on his facial expression, it was a sensation he had never felt—or been forced to feel—before, either.

As she watched him hold his glowing groin, Llenn leaped upon him from behind and jabbed her knife against the back of his defenseless neck. The foot-long blade sank into his flesh until the tip jutted from the other end.

Then she yanked it out, returned it to the sheath behind her back, and switched the P90 back to her right hand, all in one motion on fast-forward. Then she started running for the next target.

After Llenn disappeared from the screen, the man collapsed forward. He fell smack on his face, but he wouldn't have felt anything. A DEAD marker flashed over his head.

"That's...four," one person mumbled in the suddenly quiet bar.

                        *   *   *

Only two more!

Llenn raced along the wall of the house, its tattered wall racing past in her left peripheral vision.

There were no enemies in sight now. Once she turned the corner ahead, they would be there. Just as she was wondering whether she should leap out or stop, they made her decision for her.

Aw, thanks.

They came around the bend, just the muzzle of an M16A3 visible around the edge.

No matter where you are, make sure the barrel of your gun doesn't point out, Llenn, flashed Pitohui's voice inside her head.

Llenn hit the brakes and reached out with her empty left hand.

The man had switched his gun to his left shoulder, but it was a terrible mistake that he let the end of it peek around the corner. The bar crowd watching from the overhead view could see this quite well.

A hand reached around the corner and pulled the barrel as though ushering him down into Hell, yanking him off-balance.

"That's five…"

All he saw was the business end of a P90.

Prrrat! went the quick burst of fire. It was impossible to tell from the screen whether the man saw its flash of light or closed his eyes in fear.

The pink killing machine pushed the dead man with the ravaged face and leaped over his body. In the next moment, a heavy blast cried out, and a multitude of bullets scraped off the pavement in front of the house.

The last man was the one with the M37 shotgun.

He was shooting double-aught buck hunting shells with nine 8 mm lead pellets contained in each shot. These and the single-projectile slug were the cornerstones of combat-use shotguns.

As with that sort of gun, the bullets spread as they went, but the man's first shot completely missed Llenn. He engaged the pump action with a hefty *cha-kunk*, expelling the used shell and loading the next. He aimed at the small pink blur speeding sideways—but when he pulled the trigger, she was no longer there.

Llenn crossed the five-yard path in an instant and hid behind the adjacent house. She was so fast, she practically warped there. The shotgun blast punched a few holes in the house's wall.

Cha-kunk!

He pumped the shotgun again.

Conk, colla-colla-colla.

The empty shell clattered on the ground and rolled.

"That guy with the shotgun's pretty good," said someone in the crowd at the bar. Others murmured in agreement.

In real life and in *GGO*, shotguns were powerful weapons at close range. This was, naturally, because they shot multiple projectiles in a spread formation.

A shotgun's bullet circle was like some kind of magical summoning circle, a round blob that expanded and shrank. Its warning indicator to other players was a multitude of bullet lines that appeared all at once.

Each single pellet didn't do as much damage as a pistol round—the scary part was when they all hit at once. They would buffet the opponent's entire body and throw them entirely off-balance. And if the attacker kept shooting while the opponent was trying to recover, it was quite often that they died without ever getting the chance to shoot back.

Shotguns' effective range was short, usually around fifty yards, depending on the type of shells. The man and Llenn were obviously much closer than that.

His M37 had been modified so that the tube magazine under the barrel extended all the way to the muzzle. If fully loaded, it could shoot eight shells. He'd already shot one into the house, so there were five left.

And the M37 had the ability to continue engaging the pump

action as long as the trigger was held down for continuous fire. It was every bit the match of the P90 when it came to unleashing a hail of gunfire. He still had a chance.

The man knew it, too. It was why he kept aiming for where Llenn was hiding, rather than taking cover himself. The stock of the M37 was pressed to his cheek—his face displaying everything from the fear and nerves of a true battle to the delight and thrill of good competition.

"Man…this is fun."

"Which one? Which one's gonna win?"

The few seconds of madness earlier had given way to a tense, quiet confrontation. The onlookers in the bar held their breath.

Would the pink shrimp jump out and finish off the last member of the team?

Or would the shotgunner get the last shot and pull off the upset?

Each second felt like it lasted much, much longer.

Pgonk.

There was a strange sound, and the man's neck craned at a different angle. His M37 fired skyward, and the recoil jolted it out of his right hand.

He wobbled unsteadily, then toppled sideways. Llenn emerged from behind the house and trotted up to him.

Stab. She plunged her knife into his neck and killed him in a motion as quick and easy as planting the little decorative flag into the fried rice of the kid's meal at a diner. Then she put the knife back in its place, said something, and smiled. The camera rotated to what she was smiling at.

On the side of the house, a window was just slightly open, showing Fukaziroh grinning back and the deadly mouth of a 40 mm gun barrel.

"So, uh…what happened?"

On the screen, the event organizers switched to a replay for the viewers. The same footage displayed from a different angle, and then everyone understood.

Fukaziroh had crawled up to the window, opened it up, and promptly shot a grenade out of it. The projectile flew less than twenty feet.

Because it was so close, the 40 mm grenade did not explode, but the kinetic energy of its weight was enough to knock the shot-gunner's head off its axis. The grenade fell to his feet and rolled away.

"That is wicked…," someone muttered, speaking for the entire crowd.

Despite shooting bullets and slicing and stabbing with knives being so much more violent, there was something particularly painful about the idea of getting your head smashed in with a heavy object.

Llenn went back into the house, so the screen switched to another battle happening elsewhere, but all the excitement in the bar was around Llenn's team.

"Hot damn! They really are contenders! Shit, if there was a betting table set up, I'd totally put down on them!"

"And that partner…she's got some spirit! That was impressive!"

"You see how casually Llenn stabbed that guy in the neck? That's terrifying. Especially since she just looks like a little girl doing it!"

"You guys catch that? That's the power of my Llenn and her partner friend!"

"Yeah, they're pretty good. But neither of 'em are yours."

CHAPTER 7
Killed in Action

SECT.7

CHAPTER 7
Killed in Action

Slightly earlier—right around when Llenn noticed the other team setting up their ambush—battles broke out all over the map as squads selected their first targets following the Satellite Scan.

The fireworks show had only just begun.

In the hilly region north of the middle of the map, a battle was underway in a rolling valley about four hundred yards wide.

This was not a gunfight, however. It was an entirely one-sided assault.

One side was a team dressed in black and equipped with submachine guns with an effective range of two hundred yards. They were decked out like old SWAT teams, and they seemed very strong at indoor combat.

The other team had three 7.62 mm machine guns with a range of over double the valley's width, and their other two members had 5.56 mm machine guns.

"Kill 'em aaaall!"

"Hya-haaaaaaa!"

Three members of the All-Japan Machine-Gun Lovers, known by the tag of ZEMAL, settled themselves upon the slope and began blazing away. They were using an FN MAG, an M240B—these two being nearly sister models, the latter a modification of the first—and an M60E3. All were 7.62 mm caliber guns.

These were the same guns that had blasted sheets of bullets at Llenn right after the start of the first Squad Jam and hadn't hit her with a single shot.

"Hell yeah! Machine guns are awesome, man!" they cheered. The glow of their smiles mingled with the glimmering cartridges being expelled from their guns at a rapid rate.

Now, none of them had actually gone through with the nonsense idea of raising strength so they could hold two machine guns, the way they'd talked about on the phone after the first Squad Jam. But they had earned a fair amount of experience, and their accuracy was better than before.

They had also learned a new, unfamiliar word: *teamwork*.

"Okay, now a little bit to the right! Yeah, about there."

The two members with 5.56 mm guns that were just a bit too short to reach were serving as spotters. They watched through binoculars for signs of accuracy and the path of the tracer rounds, then relayed orders to the members doing the shooting.

"Awright, we got this!"

The gunners blasted away at full auto. They didn't really need to shoot that much to finish off unresisting targets, but they had yet to learn the concepts of conserving ammo or a samurai's mercy.

The team dressed in black fled in different directions up and down the valley as the curtain of bullets tore through them.

"How the hell are we supposed to win this fight?!"

But their haste to get away from the disadvantageous terrain as quickly as possible was the team's undoing. They were totally helpless.

"Dammit! If we were indoors, we wouldn't be losing this fight!"

Riddled with bullets, without a single chance to show off, the team's members toppled in quick succession, DEAD tags floating above their heads, until the entire squad was gone.

*   *   *

Meanwhile…

Another squad was busy fighting on the snowy mountains to the northeast.

Their tag was ZAT. That was an abbreviation for *Zangiri Atama no Tomo*, or "Close-Cropped Companions." It had no connection to the organization by the same acronym that protected Earth in a famous old *tokusatsu*, a live-action TV show with many special effects. It also had nothing to do with the Meiji Restoration, when the modern concept of a short haircut was first introduced to Japan.

"Enemy! We ran across the enemy while climbing the slope! According to the scan, it's MMTM, the third-place team from last time! They shot at us! Very accurately, I might add!" shouted one of the members of ZAT, who was practically buried in the snow, to an audience of one.

He was wearing brown-patterned camo, and in all directions around his helmet he had affixed tiny video cameras the size of watch batteries. His gun, entirely buried under the snow in this position, was a Type 89 5.56 mm assault rifle, the kind used by the Japan Self-Defense Force. More specifically, the folding-stock version given to the Ground SDF's airborne troops and armored division.

Only this gun and the Type 64 7.62 mm were actual Japanese assault rifles you could get in *GGO*. The Type 64 was not a popular gun, but the Type 89 was actually rather well regarded.

A benefit of these guns was that their recoil was very light, meaning it was suited to stable, accurate semi-auto fire. While they were expensive, many players found them worth the cost. And needless to say, on the Japanese server there was more than a little attachment, simply because "It's one of our guns!"

"I'm going to shoot back at them! Take that!"

The man lifted his Type 89 with one hand and let out a

three-shot burst up the slope. The bullets sprayed snow that had been stuck to the muzzle of the rifle. The Type 89, like the player, had tiny cameras stuck to it, facing forward beyond the barrel and back at the shooter.

"Did that hit them...? I can't tell at all! Man-to-man combat is very frightening! It's taking all my power to contain my bladder!" he said, his voice directed at a microphone attached to his neck.

This man with the running commentary was, sure enough, a self-styled game commentator. He would stream himself—or record a video, edit it, and upload it—playing games, which in their saved form were often called Let's Plays.

Some people would just allow the game to play out on its own, but the more clever and charismatic gamers would offer entertaining commentary and throw in funny edits and subtitles to attract viewers—just like a comedy show on TV.

Until now, this man and his friends in ZAT—who had given him permission to stream them—had fought only monsters.

As the team worked together to bring down *GGO*'s fantastic sci-fi creatures, the cameraman/commentator would film and describe what was happening, then edit the videos and upload them to the Internet. Many people did this already, but thanks to his oddly lovable personality, his videos were fairly popular.

However, he had never once uploaded a commentary video for a PvP battle.

PvP fighting could break out at any time in *GGO*, unless you agreed to a time and place beforehand. If a battle started, you couldn't upload footage of other players without their permission. It was a violation of avatar privacy. And it was obviously a huge pain to get consent from every other player in the fight.

SJ2 was a different story, though.

There was no privacy concern, because the event was already being publicly broadcast. That was with airborne cameras that didn't pick up spoken audio. But his video would be from a first-person perspective and have lots of fun commentary.

He couldn't livestream it, but there was no rule against

recording. He convinced the team to enter SJ2 so that they could take some exciting, high-impact video of a PvP battle. It hadn't gone well.

"Okay, time to see…if I can move from my position!"

Pew!

"Yikes!"

As soon as he'd raised his head, a red bullet line had appeared, quickly followed by a bullet.

"I can't do this!"

He stayed low, unable to move. He had his cheek pressed against the ground, so only sky and snow were visible. It was a good thing this was a game—he'd get frostbite otherwise.

The man had to keep up the commentary. Not because he was forced to, but it *was* the reason he was here. And because of that, he wasn't equipping his communications item. When the gunfight had started and he'd gotten separated from his teammates, he'd had no way to contact them.

Ta-ta-ta-tam. Ta-ta-ta-ta-tam.

Little bursts of gunfire like drum trills bounced off the mountainside. They didn't echo much, because the snow absorbed the sound. It simply vanished into the reddish-gray sky.

MMTM wasn't likely to waste its ammo on bad shots. He could see the HP gauge of one of his teammates dropping to zero in the upper left of his vision.

"Oh! One of my teammates just died! Benjamin! You were a good fellow! In real life, we've known each other since high school, and we've been playing games together ever since! Bennn!"

Ta-ta-tam, ta-ta-ta-ta-tam.

"Nooo! That was Casa!"

Tam, tam, tam, tam.

"Koenig! Dammit!"

Ta-ta-tam.

"Even Frost…!"

Tam.

"Yamada!"

He called out for each and every comrade who fell in battle—until he was the only one left and the leader symbol appeared next to his name.

"W-well, folks, if I don't scoot from this position soon, I'll be joining them on the list…"

The man lifted his head, and a red line instantly appeared an inch over it. The bullet zipped immediately after the line.

"Eek!"

He head-butted the snow again for cover.

"Awww…"

There was nowhere to go. He didn't even know where they were aiming from. He was trapped in place, without a single second of footage of their foes.

He narrated, "I'm speaking…to all of you…who are watching this footage… I cannot move from this spot. All my teammates have been killed. I'm not going to last much longer. I'll get shot and die soon. I'll grow cold in the snow. And all I can think about are the Popsicles I would buy and eat on the walk home from elementary school… How ironic. Man, those things were good… And yet, I never got the winning Popsicle stick that let me have another for free…"

He trailed off briefly in longing and loss.

"But maybe now I am the Popsicle stick—the winner at last!" he shouted, leaping to his feet, out of the snow, so that he could spray the area with his Type 89.

Tam! Bshk.

One well-aimed bullet caught him in the forehead, and he toppled over.

His collapse hardly made a sound.

It was all snow, anyway.

"Got 'im. I think that's all of them, but Lux and Bold, you should make sure. Everyone else, stay on alert," commanded MMTM's leader from his spot behind the thick, snowy tree.

He was wearing a snow-based camo outfit he'd stashed in his inventory, just in case. It was a white parka with green patterns that mimicked conifer needles.

He switched out the magazine of his assault rifle, a Steyr STM-556. This was a clone—essentially the same gun—of the AR-15 made by the venerable European manufacturer Steyr Mannlicher.

The AR-15 was also the basis of the M16 and the M4A1. These were used so widely by military personnel and civilians that every company had to have its own clone on the market.

They weren't exact copies, of course; each one made its mark with slight improvements, modifications that suited the times, and so on.

The STM-556 had its own unique feature. You could switch its barrels on the fly without needing to use tools or dismantle it.

A long barrel improved accuracy. But in close quarters, a longer gun was harder to use. If you needed to swing the gun around quickly, a short barrel was a vast improvement, as long as you weren't shooting long distances.

That meant shooters normally had to choose one and live with the consequences, but the STM-556 had the benefit of versatility. You just had to carry around both a long barrel and a short one and keep the other in your pack.

At the moment, the leader's STM-556 featured a long barrel for sniping. He had the small scope atop the barrel set at high magnification to function as a mid-distance sniper rifle. It was how he had hit the commentator so accurately from a considerable range.

If they got into interior combat, he would pull his short barrel out of his inventory and switch it in. Then he would put the scope back to zero magnification (in short, just a glass tube) for wider vision.

The leader's STM-556 also had a wide tube below the barrel. This was a grenade launcher, a combination weapon that could be used along with the rifle. It was easily removable by loosening a few screws.

Unlike Fukaziroh's MGL-140, it could shoot only one grenade at a time, but even that was a big boost to attack power. It had been a bold purchase specifically for the sake of SJ2. He even practiced trading off between shooting with the rifle and judiciously using the launcher.

There was only one reason for all of this: to finish off the speedy pink shrimp and the giant who'd hid behind the shield in their fateful battle at the lakeshore in the first Squad Jam.

He'd dreamed of getting into the Bullet of Bullets, *GGO's* greatest arena, worked on his skills, and finally made that dream come true—but he'd never dreamed that he'd then be taking part in some obscure little event like this.

Or that he'd be so fired up about it.

The last one had been just a simple test, a chance for his squad to do a little group training and have some fun along the way. It was thanks to the pink shrimp and the giant that he felt so ferociously enthusiastic about it now.

I'm counting on you, he mouthed to his favorite gun.

"Found six bodies. All neutralized."

"No signs of hostiles."

His teammates reported their findings.

The leader looked up. Under the cloudy sky was a field of snow, and a vast battleground was beyond it. He could see the mysterious dome, the town beyond it, and the walls that trapped them inside in the distance.

It was time to fight.

He would believe in his teammates, himself, and his gun.

"We'll wait for the next scan, then head down the mountain along the north wall. Be on alert as you move. Pull out your spare magazines now while you can."

Meanwhile, in the southwest area of the map, SHINC was in the middle of a heated battle.

"Machine guns! Keep up the pressure! Do it like we practiced!"

They were in the southern part of the town. It was farther from the station, so the houses were fewer and farther between, with plenty of empty lots and parking areas. The fortress walls loomed right overhead to the south and west behind the straight train tracks.

There were four rails spaced far apart from one another atop the gray ballast. There were multiple lines with enough space that trains could go both directions. And across that flat, open space of 160 feet, Rosa the badass mom gunner was blasting her deep, percussive PKM.

"Come get some!"

Blam, blam, blam, blam! Blam, blam! Blam, blam, blam, blam!

She was firing from the cover of the roof of an overturned freight car at an enemy team hiding among the houses on the other side of the tracks. It was the first battle for both sides.

Behind Rosa crouched Sophie the dwarf. She had a spare ammo box in hand, ready for when her partner ran out of bullets.

"Whaaa—?"

In the bar, where the patrons were watching this scene through the camera, one man paused in confusion, beer mug held in one raised hand. His friend in the next seat asked him what was up between bites of beef jerky.

"That Amazon machine gunner—not the one shooting now, but the really squat one. She had a PKM last time around, too, right?"

"Huh? Yeah."

"But she ain't got nothin' right now."

On the screen, Rosa was the only one blasting away with her machine gun. Sophie was entirely in a support role now, with no visible weapons. Perhaps she had set her gun down nearby so that it wouldn't get in the way. But from what the audience could see on-screen, that didn't seem to be the case.

"She must not have materialized it yet. It's still in her inventory," said the boy munching on jerky. He thought that nothing else seemed to make sense.

"But why? Why would she put herself at a disadvantage that way?" wondered the man drinking beer, utterly mystified.

Nobody in the bar could give him the true answer.

Rosa's hail of bullets ripped through a fence that separated the yards of two houses.

"Huh? Wait, no—"

They landed in the body and head of a character who was hiding there.

The red bullet lines had eerily passed through the fence, but he hadn't paid them any attention. If bullets were powerful enough to pass through weaker obstacles like thin boards or plants, the lines would dutifully pass through them as well.

"Shit!"

Another man, who'd just seen his teammate get killed, ran for his life, squeezing his SSG 69 bolt-action sniper rifle. He'd been on the move, hoping to flank the enemy, but now he was in danger of them firing in his vicinity.

He was a sniper, and he wore green fatigues with a special camouflage-netting item on his head and shoulders called an assault ghillie.

A full ghillie suit, which was puffy and bulky, was excellent for hiding, but it hindered mobility. For anyone but stationary snipers who didn't need to move much, the assault ghillie was much easier to manage, while still providing a good camouflage effect. Especially in Squad Jam, where you didn't have the luxury of picking your terrain.

The man even had his face painted in camo. He ran at full speed behind the wall, terrified of the machine-gun bullets that might come bursting through at any moment.

The hit point bars in his upper left vision showed three squadmates dead but two others still in perfect health. He shouted to them through his comm, "They got three of us! I'm the only one left! They knew we were behind the fence! Watch out—it's like they've got eyes in the sky! Let's regroup! Where are you?"

"B-beside that truck!"

"Got it! I'll come up from the west. Don't shoot me!"

"Roger that! Shit, those Amazons are tough! The sniper bullet lines are scary as shit! You can't poke your head out! I used to love Dragunovs, but not anymore!" the first teammate said.

From next to him, the remaining member lamented, "Let's just split! We can't do this with only three!"

"No whining! We jumped into this fight knowing they were tough! It's a battle royale, so you're bound to run across 'em eventually!"

"But..."

One of their voices stopped unnaturally.

Then the other one said, "Huh? Hey, wha—?" and stopped, too.

"..."

The man prayed that his imagination's worst-case scenario wasn't true, and he ran three more seconds, head down, around the side of a house ahead of him.

He couldn't see anyone yet. Quickly, he hung his SSG 69 on a sling and pulled his Beretta Px4 9 mm automatic pistol from his right holster. He cocked the hammer with his thumb, then steadied his grip with both hands.

"..."

Slowly, carefully, he proceeded out from the cover of the house. Then he spotted his teammates slumped next to an overturned cargo truck, DEAD markers hanging over them. He checked the bars at the side of his vision to confirm that he was the only survivor, not that he really needed the confirmation.

He had an idea of how the two were shot dead so close to him without a sound. It was the gun that had been so deadly the last time around.

"Shit! That gorilla woman...," the man swore.

"Yeah, that's me. You're the only one left, I assume," said a woman, right nearby.

"Wha—?!"

He spun around with the Px4—first directly behind him, then left and right.

But there were no living characters in the vicinity. Yet, he heard her speak very clearly. There was only one possibility.

"Are you...using one of our comms?" he asked the unseen enemy.

"That's right. I'm just testing it out. I wanted to know if you could grab it off the body and use it. You can use their guns and grenades up to the end of the battle, so why not their phones?"

In other words, she had taken it from the first teammate killed, then overheard all his commands and conversation, making it child's play for her to kill his other teammates. And now he was next.

"Damn, that's not cool." He chuckled.

A bullet sped toward him.

It hit his right eye and burst out of the back of his head.

Fifty yards away, Boss looked down through the scope of her silenced Vintorez sniper rifle and pulled it away from the open window of the house.

"I have to agree," she admitted to the man she'd just killed. "Sorry."

Around the same time that this merciless battle was happening, two squads were busy with a very odd fight at the giant bridge on the eastern side of the map.

Both sides were six-man teams with 5.56 mm assault rifles, and they were locked in battle on the highway atop the bridge. It was a straight road over a mile and a quarter in length. There wasn't a single abandoned vehicle over its four lanes—it was perfectly clear. The bridge hung over three hundred feet above the valley floor.

In other words, the bridge was its own battlefield, without obstacles to hide behind or cover for shelter from bullets, and there was no escape to either side. It was just a flat, empty, elongated space over a hundred feet wide.

Two teams attempting to cross the valley from opposite directions had learned that the other was just ahead, thanks to the scan. They could've chosen to pull back, but instead they charged forward in search of battle, found their foes in the middle of the bridge, and were now engaged in a firefight at a distance of five hundred yards.

However, *GGO* had bullet lines. Opponents knew where the bullets would go, so they could duck, leap, and tumble to avoid a shot if necessary. It was even easier knowing that the enemy was far away, straight ahead.

No one could shoot if they were dodging all the time, so as soon as the line vanished, they would set up and aim back, only for the other side to avoid it the same way. But now if they wanted to turn back to the end of the bridge, they wouldn't be able to see the lines, and they'd get shot in the back. If they tried to back up while facing forward, the other team might take that opportunity to race after them and close the gap.

So both teams instead persisted in pushing forward. *We'll inch onward and finally land a shot!*

They probably should have given up on that.

Instead, their battle turned into a strange game of Red Light, Green Light, where each side took turns dancing out of the way of incoming shots and aiming at the other side.

This confrontation was caught on camera and shown on one of the monitors in the bar.

"Oh, geez. This is what you get for trying to cross the bridge without a plan."

"I'm an idiot, and I feel qualified to state that these people are also idiots."

The crowd was not impressed. Naturally, this skirmish wasn't going to win over the viewers of Llenn's and Boss's battles. The onlookers left that monitor for more exciting fare, and the viewers in their private booths changed the channel.

While the squads atop the bridge tussled, there was a character close to death in the south-middle part of the map, surrounded by barren fields and trees that had lost all their leaves.

The man had bullet wounds on his chest and face, and before his HP could completely drop to zero, he shouted, "I couldn't see it! I never saw any bullet li—!"

He toppled to the dry earth before he could finish his sentence and went still, a DEAD tag floating over his body.

There were two other bodies in the wide, empty field—as well as three men still alive, hiding in a row in a dried-up waterway.

This squad wore uniforms and gear similar to that of historical armies. There was an American Green Beret from the Vietnam War era, a Russian Airborne Troops soldier from the Soviet War in Afghanistan, a mercenary from the Rhodesian Bush War, a West German soldier from the Cold War, and at the oldest, an English infantryman and an Imperial Japanese officer from World War II.

Naturally, they used only guns that matched their designated historical settings. Some of them were so old that it came as a surprise they were in *GGO* at all.

These guys loved military history. They strove to wear period-accurate attire—a squadron dedicated to nostalgia in the future world of *GGO*.

In their own headcanon, they were soldiers assumed dead during various historical conflicts who had actually been sent to the future through some mysterious power and now worked as a team in the hopes that they might one day find their way back home.

They ironically chose the name New Soldiers for their squad. As was the standard procedure, this got abbreviated to the tag NSS for Squad Jam's purposes. In their first Squad Jam, they started in the woods on the southern part of the map.

The 1:10 scan told them they were surrounded by many enemy teams, most notable of which was SHINC, the previous runners-up, to their west. The New Soldiers avoided them by charting a course north, choosing the KKHC team there to be their first opponent. They had no knowledge of this team, but surely they would be easier foes than the foreboding Amazons.

It was a risky move to pass through the flat, open farmland, but they had little choice. They made their way across the dry, dusty earth, scanning the horizon with binoculars all the while.

If anyone got sniped, the rest would hit the deck. As you couldn't detect the location of the first shot ahead of time, there was no way to dodge it if it happened.

Sure enough, they got sniped.

The West German soldier with the G3A3ZF and the English infantryman with the Lee Enfield No. 4 Mk. I (T) were shot in the chest and face and immediately died. The sound of their bodies hitting the dirt overlapped with the arrival of the distant gunshots.

The other four took cover in the dried-out waterway and made sure they identified the location of the enemy. They'd seen the muzzle flash, so they knew where their foe was: according to the range finder, a narrow little copse of trees hardly more than sixty feet to a side, at a distance of 1,437 feet.

It hurt to lose two members right away—and their own snipers, at that—but there was no resurrection magic in *GGO*, so they'd have to make do. The other team had probably identified them as snipers and taken them out first on purpose. But now they knew where to find their foe.

The enemy within that thicket couldn't move from the spot now. If they tried to run, they'd have to move out into the open.

Now all the New Soldiers needed to do was creep forward, avoiding the bullet lines, until they could attack.

Fortunately, the Soviet soldier's AKS-74 assault rifle had an attached grenade launcher. Once they reached his maximum effective range of 1,300 feet, he could blast the woods with grenades from a safe, prone position.

They only had to close less than 150 feet. If they could reach the next waterway over, victory would be within their grasp.

The Green Beret, the team's leader and quickest member, said, "I'll go first. Don't bother with covering fire—it's just a waste of ammo. Here goes!"

He leaped forward, XM177E2 assault rifle in one hand. His squadmates popped their heads up to watch, hoping to see him nimbly dodge the bullet lines and race onward heroically.

In three seconds, he was dead.

And his dying message was "I couldn't see it! I never saw any bullet li—!"

The other three sank into terror.

They hunched their heads down in the dry waterway, jabbering into their comms.

"Wh-wh-what the hell does that mean? Why couldn't he see it? Is it a bug?" demanded the FAL-wielding Rhodesian mercenary.

"No, that can't be it… I've never heard of that happening before. Plus, I was close by, and I didn't see it, either," insisted the Soviet.

"But there's no way Leader would miss that! Not when he's sober!"

The Green Beret had a habit of logging in drunk and being a pain in the ass for his squadron, but he was dry today. The West German soldier, who was his friend in real life, had made absolutely certain the previous night that there had been no drinking.

"Then…there's only one possibility," said the Imperial Japanese soldier calmly, his Type 100 submachine gun in hand.

"What's that?"

"He's shooting without a line, with his own innate knowledge and skill. You can do that if you leave your finger off the trigger until you pull. It's not cheating."

"Yeah, but…are you saying he aimed from that distance without the system helping and scored a headshot on the first try?"

"He's just that good of a shot. Meaning…"

Meaning? The other two waited.

"He's too tough for us to handle right now. We can't get any farther this way. Let's turn back east," he concluded. *Turn back* sounded nice, but it was actually a euphemism for *retreat.*

How did the other two feel about running away in the face of the enemy with half of their team already dead?

"Sounds good."

"Yeah, I agree."

The New Soldiers left a trio of dead behind and crawled away. "Heavens protect us."

The camera silently followed their rear ends as they went.

The sniping team hiding within the woods burst into cheers.

"We did it! Our first victory!"

"Yahoo!"

"That went really well!"

"I guess we can do this after all!"

The men were exultant beyond what the situation warranted. It was as though they'd just knocked a piece of candy off the shelf at the festival shooting gallery.

They were flat against the ground behind a shrub in the patch of woods. The only parts of them visible were the tips of their long boots and the ends of their rifles. All four of them had long, protruding barrels, which, given the distance of the shots, had to be sniper rifles.

"You could've tried shooting, too, Shirley," one of the men said.

"No, I'm fine. You enjoy," said a woman's voice, presumably

belonging to Shirley. "I'm going to watch. It's quite possible that they ran off."

"You sure? You're gonna get shot," warned some nearby unseen person.

"If I do, I do," Shirley replied, rustling out from under the shrub and crawling backward on her hands and knees. She emerged feetfirst, leaving her gun behind.

Like the others in her squad, she wore long, galosh-like boots and cargo pants. Her belt held a large magazine pouch on her right side and a nasty curved knife called a *ken-nata*.

On top, she wore a jacket with a detailed camouflage look called the Realtree pattern, which utilized actual images of trees and dead leaves and such. On her head was a baseball cap in the same pattern, turned backward so the brim wouldn't hit her scope.

The look was perfect for this kind of environment. It was as though her upper half were completely transparent. While that part of her practically vanished into the shrub, her pale face and the bit of hair that stuck out from the cap were quite striking. Especially that bright-green hair—the color of brand-new leaves.

Shirley's expression was the dictionary definition of *disgruntled*. She'd be quite pretty if she smiled, but at the moment, she wore a scowl that would send any man running. And this was after her comrades had won the battle and started celebrating to their hearts' content.

Once she was completely upright, she hid behind a tree. Then she looked through a small pair of binoculars hanging over her shoulder at the looming wall and vast fields ahead for five seconds or so.

"The other three are running to the mountain. I only see their hats here and there. Pretty far off now. Can't see anyone else," she reported.

The rest of her team chimed in.

"Darn… Over so soon!"

"They ran off in fear! We utterly dominated the first battle!"

"That was easy!"

"I wanted to shoot more!"

Shirley sighed heavily.

"Hey, given our skill, you think we might actually get pretty far in this?" one of them continued.

"Yeah, I bet. It's gonna be a bloodbath."

"You really need to have practice shooting in real life!"

Then Shirley finally decided to reach up and switch off the comm device in her ear. She turned her back to her comrades.

"Is it really that fun to shoot people with guns? You're all crazy. I hope you all get shot already. Then this stupid tournament will end," she muttered under her breath.

*　　　*　　　*

Plenty of people weren't being televised on the monitors, because they weren't currently in battle. One such person included Pitohui, who let loose her innermost feelings.

"I'm so bored!"

She was in an area of rocks and woods on the slope of the southeast mountain, sitting on a fallen tree trunk. Over her navy-blue suit, she wore a camo cloak in the same pattern as M's and the other four's. With the rough, jaunty way her cloak sat on her shoulders, and her right knee crossed sideways over her left, she looked like some proud, confident samurai general of the past.

Her hands were empty. She held no rifle, not even a pistol.

Nearby, M and the other four were watching the surrounding area cautiously. Through the rustling of the branches, the wind brought sounds of faint, very distant gunfire.

The slopes were steep all around them, nothing but thick conifer trees and craggy rocks. Visibility was poor here.

M was peering through the trees and down the mountainside with his binoculars, his M14 EBR at his side. His huge shield-holding backpack was turned around to cover his stomach, to protect him from snipers.

The four other members, with their faces hidden, had their gear out now. Like M, they all wore thick bulletproof vests. The trio of a short man, a tall man, and a fat man were scattered throughout the trees, and whatever weapons they had brought out to carry weren't visible from here.

The last member of PM4, a skinny man, was waiting just behind Pitohui. Hanging from his right hip was a Glock 21 .45-caliber pistol. His hands were empty.

"Say, M, why are we just wasting time around here? Everyone else is shooting bad guys. There's plenty of them down there, so why aren't we rushing down the mountain right now?" Pitohui demanded through the comm with little concern.

M answered, "We can't."

"Why not? M, are you telling me…you don't want to fight? Are you being a big chicken like last time?" she teased. M didn't fall for it.

"It's a strategy."

"Ooh, a strategy. What do the rest of you think?"

The four men must have heard her, but none of them replied right away.

Eventually one said, "We take our orders from the leader. That's in the contract." The others chimed in with affirmatives.

"Oh. I see," Pitohui replied, clearly unhappy. She didn't scold them for being uptight, though.

M continued, "There's no need to take part in the mindless rush at the start. You want to die that way? That's how you want it to happen?"

"What?! Well, no, but this is lame. It's so boring."

"You'll have to put up with it for a bit. As I said, this is a strategy, Pito. You asked me to be the team leader, and that means you have to follow my lead."

"Tsk! Fine, I guess I have to. But if you die, then I get to be the leader, and I'll do what I want," Pitohui declared, raising her hands to the sky theatrically. There were no cameras there.

"Don't worry. Whatever powerful enemies are still surviving at the end of this, I'll let you brave their deadly fangs."

"Like who?"

"Like Llenn, perhaps. The pink rabbit's fangs are sharp, indeed."

"Ha-ha!"

It was fortunate for the viewers that the cameras weren't capturing the ferocious smile on Pitohui's lips.

CHAPTER 8
Different Plans

SECT.8

CHAPTER 8
Different Plans

Between 1:10 and 1:19, eighteen of the thirty teams engaged in battle.

Seven of them were either wiped out entirely or resigned because they found it futile to continue. The two teams jockeying on top of the bridge opted for the latter. At the time of the second Satellite Scan, twenty-three teams remained.

Of course, some of those surviving teams had suffered significant casualties that put them at a major disadvantage. They would be forced to consider how they intended to continue competing.

There was just one team that had only two members from the start.

"Yes! I grew feet! Yaaay!"

Fukaziroh had full freedom of movement again. They were in a different house than the one they'd first run into for shelter. Llenn had had to drag her friend so far to get there that she'd been afraid she would seriously hurt her back.

Enough time had passed since Fuka's injury that the glowing red spots of her severed feet had grown into new feet, like magic. This was definitely a video game, all right. Even the tights and boots that had gotten blown off were back.

She'd used a med kit while waiting for her new feet, so her HP had steadily recovered almost to the maximum.

"Hya-hoo! My feet! I love having feet!" Fukaziroh exclaimed, hopping around the room.

"Perfect!"

Llenn was at the window, looking outside for signs of hostiles. She checked her watch. The digital readout, which adjusted its brightness automatically for the darkened room, read 1:19:20.

"We'll check the next scan from here," she announced. There wasn't time to go anywhere else.

"Aye, aye! And I won't goof up like that again! I'm gonna stare right down where I'm walking! And I'll tell 'em, 'We've come a long way, babies'!"

"Sure. Just be aware that those trip wires can be placed at your waist or your head level, too. Or even at a height that's just enough that you think you can step over it, but you end up touching. Some of them are even double trapped, where trying to disarm the first one sets off another."

"Yikes. That's brutal." Fukaziroh grimaced, but Llenn just grinned back.

"That's combat in *GGO*. You'll get used to it. In fact, it'll get to the point that you start checking doorways for wires even in real life."

"Look at how tough and self-sufficient you are now... I'm so proud of you."

The second Satellite Scan commenced.

This satellite came directly from the south at a quick pace. The scan buzzed across the map, forcing Llenn and Fukaziroh to observe the dots in a rush. They saw that seven teams had lost or resigned.

"Yes!"

"Still there."

Pitohui's team was alive and well. They'd hardly moved from their starting position, and there were no defeated- or resigned-team dots nearby. That suggested they hadn't engaged anyone yet.

"That's good to know...but it's still a long trip over there," Llenn murmured, conflicted.

Their target was still far across the map from their current location in the town, and a number of glowing dots stood between them.

The closest one indicated a squad was at the train station, less than two-thirds of a mile away. Zooming in on the map placed the dot right in the middle, where the platform would be, but that was as close as Llenn and Fukaziroh could see.

They could tell that the other team wasn't on the move. Since the scan did indicate direction of movement, it was typical for teams to stay still if at all possible. You couldn't avoid that if you were on the run from another group, however, and for the duration of the scan, some people even utilized a high-level technique of moving only in a certain direction that was counter to their true destination, just to throw off potential hunters.

Llenn considered why they might be at the station for a few moments, using all the knowledge she'd gleaned from Pitohui and M. She concluded, "The tracks go north and south from here, but there's a rotary around the station to the east and west. It's got to have some of the best visibility of the entire town area. If the platform's made of concrete, it'll be thick enough to stand firm against bullet penetration. They're probably setting up between the tracks and lying in wait."

Fukaziroh was furious. "More ambushes?! These cowards! I'm going to squash them with a train!"

But, much like the intentional walk in baseball, that was a perfectly acceptable strategy. Same as the group earlier.

After her championship run last time, Llenn's skill in terms of speed, size, and lack of mercy was a well-known factor to the audience watching. Naturally, any team entering the event would decide that they'd have better chances against her if they waited in a defensible spot with good visibility, instead of hoping for a chaotic close-quarters scuffle.

It seemed to her that Fukaziroh's plan to *squash them with a train* wouldn't be a bad one, but that assumed any trains you might find would actually run, and she certainly wasn't an engineer.

The map revealed that SHINC was still alive, too. They'd

crossed the tracks and moved northeast since the last scan. There was one gray dot along their route—clearly the girls' work.

"…"

Oh no.

Llenn frowned. If Boss and her team continued on their route, the two groups would run into each other around the dome in the middle of the map, or perhaps before the mountain to the southeast. It seemed like SHINC could've just come straight north to meet up, but there was no use whining about it.

Argh! Don't get passive now! That just leads to defeat! Llenn scolded herself. She had told herself the plan earlier: eliminate all in her way.

The scan was over within thirty seconds. Llenn put away her device and told her partner, "The station team's in our way, so we're gonna beat them! We'll approach by sneaking from house to house."

Fukaziroh smiled. It was supposed to be a pure, innocent girl's smile, but in the darkened room and with her devilish features, it appeared more like she was plotting something.

"Say, Llenn, as an apology for screwing up the last time, I wanna do more of the heavy lifting this fight."

"Okay. You got any ideas?"

"Yeah. In fact, I'll wipe the station team out before you even need to fire a shot."

After the 1:20 scan, the other teams checking the map assessed their situations and made their plans.

Boss and SHINC were outside of the town and nearly to the farm fields. They proceeded onward on foot, wary of the increase in visibility and vulnerability. Anna and Tohma, the two snipers, kept an eye out through their binoculars, but they knew from the scan that no teams were close enough to run into in the next ten minutes—unless a team leader was left somewhere as bait and the rest of the squad members were hiding elsewhere on the map.

"They ran off…," Boss murmured.

People knew about their level of skill, so everyone in their vicinity scampered directly away like baby spiders leaving the egg sac. Everybody had the same idea: let the contenders fight other squads first and get softened up a bit.

"Hey, you slugs! Don't any of you have any balls?!" shouted Boss at their unseen opponents.

"Oh my. Such vulgar language," Sophie teased over her shoulder.

Boss spun around and said, "Why can't I say that in a game? It's just role-playing." Yet, in this moment, the teenager was clearly visible behind the character.

"If you want, but if you get carried away, you might slip up and say something like that in real life. Like when we're all riding on the subway!"

"Ugh! Yeah, that would be...bad."

"Right? So let's try that one again. Like a proper mature woman this time."

"All right," Boss agreed. She turned back to the open fields and addressed their unseen opponents with more civility this time.

"Gentlemen, have you no testicles?"

Team MMTM watched the scan from a snowy field near the northern wall.

They still wore their white parkas and remained stationary with their lower halves buried in the snow, so their camouflage was perfect. Opponents wouldn't be able to pick them out in a picture as long as they stayed still.

Their leader formulated a plan as he watched the scan.

LF and SHINC were still alive. Obviously, they weren't going to get knocked out that easily. PM4 was still around, too; they had barely moved.

He wanted to fully enjoy the battle and throw the team into a direct confrontation with one of them, but that would be too hasty at this point. The event's producers, in the hope of making it more exciting, had really screwed with the spirit of battle.

"Got no choice. We have to move west," he ordered.

While each team had its own plans, there was one that had a completely different idea than any of the others.

They were at the foot of the mountain where Pitohui's squad was hanging out, staring up at its impressive rocks and trees. When the scan showed them that a number of teams were near the farm area, one member, a man wearing a bunch of bulky protectors, told the others, "It's about time. Let's carry out the plan!"

Then he told them, "I'm going to check again with you one last time. Once we start this strategy, there's no going back. Any objections?"

He received unanimous assent from his companions.

"Good! Then prepare the white flag! Let's put Operation Platoon into motion."

✳   ✳   ✳

1:25 PM.

Llenn and Fukaziroh zipped through the ghost town at full speed until they neared the train station. Naturally, they adjusted their pace as they approached, preparing for the possibility that the team at the station might come out in search of combat.

"Okay, nobody here."

The ambush team had not taken the battle to them.

Under the gloomy sky, Fukaziroh squatted behind a general store located about three hundred yards northwest of the station. The windows of the shop featured English signs that blazed GOING-OUT-OF-BUSINESS SALE FOR THE WHOLE PLANET! MAKE THE LAST SHOPPING TRIP OF YOUR LIFE WITH US!

"Looks good. Let's use this place."

Up ahead were a number of small businesses of a similar size and the station traffic rotary. If they went farther, they'd fall within the ambush team's range and suffer a hail of bullets.

While *range* could mean a number of different distances

depending on what kind of gun the player used, this was about right for your average 5.56 mm assault rifle. Any closer and they'd be putting themselves in danger.

"Tell me the direction, Llenn."

"Roger that."

Llenn moved quickly up to the house and peered around the side, just long enough to spot the tracks, rotary, and station, and then pulled back again. She pointed with her left hand for Fukaziroh's benefit.

"This way. About three hundred yards."

"Okay, cool. Got it. I can handle it from here."

Fukaziroh lowered one of her two MGL-140s to the ground and sat down, her legs splayed in front of her. She leaned back until her large backpack held her torso up, then she cradled the MGL-140 between her thighs and pointed it up into the sky.

"Okay, Llenn, take it away." Fukaziroh grinned.

"Okay, Fuka, take it away," Llenn returned, patting her partner's shoulder and taking off at a run.

Once upon a time, the train station had been a valuable source of public transport for the people of this run-down little town. Even now, after its inhabitants had gone, it sat comfortably at rest.

The Western-style station sign was too dirty and dilapidated to read, and it sagged at a diagonal angle. Red rust covered the tracks, the ties desiccated and split from the ends. The station building itself was as simple as a small house, located on the east side of the tracks. It had collapsed in the middle, as though the central load-bearing pillar had split.

The platforms themselves, made of sturdy concrete, were still in good shape. There were two of them bordering the two sets of tracks, making four rails in total.

The team had prepared their base amid the platforms and atop the tracks. The platforms were about two feet tall, shorter than the ones in Japan. Six players hunched between them.

They were all men, and their outfits were varied. Some had very precisely picked camo gear, some wore futuristic battle outfits in keeping with the setting, and some looked completely normal in jeans and track jackets, like they were out running errands.

They also shared one thing in common that no other team did: All their weapons were light guns, the fictional sci-fi weapons that shot beams of compressed light energy. Most people avoided them in PvP settings because defensive fields cut down on most of their power, but this team had specifically chosen them for use in SJ2.

The biggest benefit of these weapons was that the team didn't have to worry about ammo. Optical guns ran on energy packs similar to batteries, rather than magazines stuffed with bullets. The number of shots you could take with one pack was far beyond the amount possible with one live-ammo magazine.

Another benefit of optical guns was their light carrying weight, meaning the team could bring many more guns with them. There were two machine-gun-type weapons, large and bulky, with high-capacity energy packs for long-term continuous fire; one sniper-rifle type with its own scope; four that would be classified as assault rifles; three submachine-gun types for close-range battle; and six pistol types.

It was quite an arsenal, which would allow them to adapt to any situation. And after the last scan, they had set up in an advantageous defensive position to wait for LF, the team with one of the previous champions on it.

1:28.

In the distance, there was a quiet *pomp* sound.

"What was that? Did somebody fart?" asked the track-jacket guy with the sniper-rifle type of light gun. The other five laughed.

Then a grenade landed near the station where the six of them were taking shelter.

The grenade exploded near the center of the traffic rotary, about a hundred feet from the squad, emitting a loud burst and a wave of shrapnel. A few pieces sprinkled harmlessly on the distant head of a man using his binoculars. He didn't take any damage.

"Yikes! That was a grenade! Watch out!" he shouted, ducking his head.

"Calm down—that was way off. They're just shooting at random based on the results of the scan. Just like the Amazons shooting their machine guns in the video of the last Squad Jam—they're trying to rustle us out. Don't panic—they'll have another team approaching separately. Do not fire until you spot the enemy. We're in an overwhelmingly advantageous position. There is no reason for us to leave it," commanded their apparent leader, a man in camo with an optical machine gun.

"Oh…okay…"

"Don't worry. We're not going to lose right here. Be confident. Trust in your teammates. Trust in our victory. We're going to fight hard, survive this twisted, corrupt world, and carve our names into eternal glo—"

His motivational speech was so effective, and his comrades were so diligent in watching the horizon, that no one actually noticed the bullet line that descended from the sky to land right in their midst.

Pomp.

With a crisp, concussive sound, a grenade landed behind one of the men and exploded.

"Bull's-eye."

Llenn watched through her monocular as the man flew into the air, missing everything below the waist. Through the comm, she relayed, "Two more about five yards nearer on the north side."

She was speaking from a location about two hundred yards from the station, flat against the sheet-metal roof of a house, making use of the angle and the chimney so that only the lens of the monocular was visible as she watched the station through it. With its magnification at maximum, she could see the target well enough, and a digital readout on her scope told her the distance.

"Roger that," came Fukaziroh's reply. A few seconds later, a grenade exploded in the spot indicated. One of the two panicked men suffered vicious shrapnel wounds, his whole body glowing red. Llenn saw it happen, then heard the explosion a moment later. It was like distant fireworks.

Fukaziroh's strategy was simple.

From a fixed position, she would aim her grenades to land in the midst of the enemies at the station. There were plenty of houses in between, so they wouldn't be able to see her.

Meanwhile, Llenn would watch the station from a safe location and relay her instructions and feedback on the bombing. After the first blind shot, Llenn would just tell her how far away she was and in what direction she needed to shoot.

"And is that...going to be accurate?" Llenn wondered doubtfully.

"Good question. How much time do you think I spent practicing this while you weren't online?"

"A whole lot..."

"Staring your enemy in the eyes isn't the only part of battle. I knew that these guns were going to make this strategy possible. So I practiced measuring distances and hitting targets on instinct alone. At this point, I can hit someone with a grenade with my eyes closed, just knowing the exact distance—and with accurate directions, of course."

"Okay...I'm in. But you'll be stuck in place and defenseless, Fuka."

"I should've died once already. Nobody's supposed to feel sorry for the zombie!"

"Two men on the ground, sixty feet closer."

"Gotcha. I'll shoot two."

A few seconds later, consecutive grenades landed. They exploded about ten feet to the left and right of the men who tried to evacuate with their optical guns in hand—and that was the end of them.

"Back to the track, one hundred sixty feet. One target running."

"Okay, I'll get him. Two shots."

A grenade exploded right before the fleeing man, and while he took some shrapnel damage, it wasn't serious, and he merely dropped where he was. The second grenade landed smack on his back. His body split into over a dozen pieces—the glimmering damage effect was like red mist.

"Hit. One left. Running dead east across the platform. We can let him go, but I'd like to finish him off."

"Then I'll use up all the rest!"

Pomp-pomp-pomp-pomp-pomp-pomp!

Fukaziroh had switched to her second MGL-140, and she let loose all its ammo in one go.

The last man took off running. He ran through the rotary on the east side of the station like some kind of action hero, explosions going off left and right around him. Eventually, he dived behind a dilapidated car, blocking him from Llenn's view.

Then the sixth and final grenade exploded on the other side of the car. Llenn saw only a severed hand fly into the air, faithfully holding the man's optical gun.

A DEAD tag appeared, half-visible over the top of the car.

"Okay…that's all of them, Fuka! Nicely done! Amazing! Brilliant! Bravo!" cheered Llenn heartily.

"Yeah, seems about right. I can do this!"

"Let's meet back up!"

Llenn put the monocular in its waist pouch and slid back down the sloped roof until she reached the edge and dropped. From there, she landed on the roof of a truck below, rolled forward, then jumped neatly onto the road. It was the reverse of the way she'd gotten up there.

Now that the "second round" of SJ2 had passed without a hitch, Llenn checked her watch. The battle had taken less than a minute.

With her superhuman speed—it would likely set a short-distance world record if she timed herself—Llenn rushed back to Fukaziroh, who was reloading her grenades.

"Let's go to the station! We'll watch the scan there and head for the dome next!"

Their journey toward Pitohui continued.

* * *

At one thirty, the third scan started from the northwest.

Llenn and Fukaziroh stood between the train platforms, in the space that had been an enemy stronghold just minutes before, watching their Satellite Scan terminals with four dead bodies scattered around them.

Boss and the other members of Team SHINC went into the woods of the farmland area and took cautious defensive positions. Only Boss was looking at the screen.

Beyond the trees, the mysterious dome rose white and menacing over the scene.

Surrounded by his squadmates among the rocks and trees, M watched his terminal. Behind him, Pitohui was in full-on relaxation mode on a softer mound of dirt she'd found.

"Just let me know if anything's different," she said without getting up.

The third scan started from the northwest. The eye from space distributed information equally to all surviving players.

As far as newly defeated teams went, one was the dot that Fukaziroh had blown clean off the train station. There were two others in the hills on the north side of the map, with the surviving team near them being MMTM. Their skill was the real deal, so it seemed clear that they'd defeated the other two in the last ten minutes.

On the east side of the town, there were three downed teams among the houses. The team that had fled from SHINC and the team that had started SJ2 in the middle of the town had been unlucky enough to gather in this region.

Given how close together the roads were at this spot, it must've been a short, tense battle. There were no other survivors nearby, so it seemed likely that they'd wiped each other out.

Lastly, the scan reached the southeast mountain where M's team was hiding.

"Hmm?"

"Whoa!"

"My goodness."

"Hmm…"

Llenn, Boss, MMTM's leader, and M reacted simultaneously across the map.

The southeast corner of the map was a steep, treacherous mountain, about a mile and a quarter on each side. The only team there was PM4, Pitohui's team, which had stayed there since the start of the battle. The other squads had run off.

But in the farm fields on the western foothill of the mountain was a collection of seven white dots. They were essentially in the same spot.

They were so close together that you had to zoom in on the map just to tell that there were a bunch of them in the same place.

"What do you suppose this means, Llenn? Seven in the same place? That doesn't seem likely, does it?" Fukaziroh wondered.

"Dammit…"

Llenn wore her most severe expression yet. She understood the situation instantly.

"What's this? That's interesting," opined Tanya, the silver-haired Bizon gunner. Her voice reached the other SHINC members through the comm, so they couldn't see her expression, but the excitement was clear in her tone.

She continued, "I definitely wouldn't play along with this tactic, though."

MMTM's leader's sole reaction was a mocking, mirthless laugh.

"Ha!"

M calmly advised, "Pito, you can still check out your device lying down. You should take a look. It's interesting."

The scan concluded.

In the last ten minutes, six teams had lost or resigned. Seventeen still remained.

Fukaziroh put away her device, lifted her MGL-140s, and wondered, "What does this mean, Llenn? If you know, explain it."

"I'll tell you as we run! Keep up!" Llenn said, rushing off with her P90 in hand. She still looked very tense.

"Roger that."

Fukaziroh followed her lead and hopped onto the train platform.

There were no enemies likely to impede their progress on the path to the dome. Two teams were inside it, but they could ignore them for now. So Llenn took off running.

Like before, she took the lead at top speed, then found cover and watched for danger as she waited for Fukaziroh to catch up. Once that happened, she darted forward again.

All the while, she explained what she had learned from the recent scan.

"Those seven squads are teaming up!"

"Huh? What do you mean?"

"I mean they've decided on a cease-fire! Their leaders were probably meeting up in person to bargain! I think someone clever must have convinced the other teams in their area to agree on a plan! They're probably going to team up together and try to tackle M's squad on the mountain with dozens of troops!"

"Ohhh! The mystery is solved!"

"What a miserable excuse for competition," observed Anna, the blond sniper.

"Pathetic worms without pride...," grumbled Boss.

They were both talking under their breath, but the comms carried their comments to the rest of the squad.

Rosa was watching the horizon with her PKM machine gun at the ready. "Do they think that if they all work together, they can beat M?"

"We'll see about that. Of course, there is superiority in numbers. No matter how good M is, that shield can't protect him from above and behind and all around, all at once," Boss conceded. She shrugged her shoulders. "We'll just have to wait for the results."

"Well, it *is* a strategy—that's for certain… I'm surprised they got all the others to play along," noted MMTM's leader. "I just wish they'd talked to us, too."

Jake, the team member with the HK21 machine gun, seemed surprised. "Huh? Are you saying we'd have gone in, too, Leader?"

"Oh, hell no," Leader said instantly. "I'd pretend to hear them out, then wipe the whole group when I got the chance. This is a battle royale! There are no allies here."

When the four men of Team KKHC—the one with green-haired Shirley—watched the scan and came away with the same conclusion as the other teams, they were thrilled. They jabbered away through their comms to one another from their very well-hidden positions in the greenery.

"It's like a big hunting party… Man, we should have taken part in it, too!"

"It's too late. We'll never make it over to group up with them in time."

"Good point… What should we do, then? What's our plan, Leader?"

"Plan…? Well, I wanna see how that fight plays out. So we'll either hide or run until then."

Shirley, the lone woman of the group, peered through the trees with her binoculars.

"…"

She didn't join the conversation; she just snorted with derision.

Llenn was running across flat ground toward the dome when she tripped and fell.

200 Sword Art Online Alternative **Gun Gale Online, Vol. 2**

"Aaah!"

Her foot had caught on a pipe, but it hadn't taken her by surprise.

The pipe was in a bothersome location, but it was lying on the ground, so she'd intended to kick it out of the way. Instead, to her surprise, it was fixed firmly in the ground. It must've been a water line of some kind to a house that had once stood in that spot.

It was such a simple and stupid mistake to make. Llenn tumbled and rolled along the ground as Fukaziroh caught up to her.

"Come on—calm down. You're getting a bit carried away here."

"Hurgh..."

Llenn came to a stop, but her eyes kept spinning. Her pink battle gear was all dusty now. Fukaziroh looked all around them, then held out a hand to pull her partner up.

"Thanks..."

"Hey, there's no use rushing."

"But—! It doesn't matter how tough Pito and M are when they're up against that many!"

"Would we even make it in time by running from here?"

"..."

If Llenn ran alone without needing to stop, she still wouldn't make it in time. She had no answer.

While keeping a wary eye out for trouble, Fukaziroh reassured her, "If their team's really that good, they should be smart enough to cut and run if they know they can't win. Don't worry about them."

"I...I hope you're right..."

Llenn stared to the southeast, praying for Pitohui's and M's safety.

But she couldn't see the mountain because the dome was in the way.

✳   ✳   ✳

Turning back the clock somewhat, the events that transpired between 1:20 and 1:30 were largely as Llenn and the others imagined them.

The team with the leader covered in bulky protectors pulled an enormous white flag out of their inventory and stood it up in a visible spot in the farmland.

It was a flag several yards tall and long, made to be legible from a long distance. It had a message written on it: *Don't shoot! We have a plan! Send someone over, and we won't harm them!*

This came as a great surprise to the other squads nearby. They were all set to attack any nearby foes, but the message caught them off guard.

At first, they were wary and confused, but when they recalled that the foreboding PM4 was on the mountain behind them, it began to make sense.

Each team sent one or two members as envoys, at which point they learned that their expectations were correct. It was a plan to band together to defeat a powerful foe—to knock PM4 and its defending champion member right out of SJ2.

After that would be MMTM or the Amazon gang. And if those two were down, LF would be next.

Once all the most powerful squads were out of the picture, they'd split apart and let the true battle royale resume. This would allow the "weaker" teams to enjoy SJ2 longer and would give them a chance at the championship or other prizes.

The man who'd proposed the idea also had a strategy in mind for tackling the big baddies. It would be the leader-decoy plan that the champions from the last Squad Jam had used. They'd bring all the team leaders into the same safe location and send the rest of their personnel on the attack.

The only thing the Satellite Scan showed was the leader's location. So they'd take advantage of that and leave only the leaders in one place. The enemy could see their dots on the scan, but they wouldn't know where the other members of the participating squads would be. It would force their enemies to fight using only what they could see with their own eyes.

Even better, they'd all have the comm units that would allow them to communicate and coordinate with their attacking members. The leaders could glance at the terrain on the map and come up with plans like, "My boys will attack from this direction, so you send yours to flank them on the other side."

That would give them numerical superiority, freedom of movement, and the advantage in strategy. Some squads jumped on the idea at once, declaring it fantastic, while others weren't so sure.

As they discussed and debated, more teams arrived, starting the negotiations fresh and bringing more people on board. And as more and more joined up, even the skeptical teams had to admit that the plan was looking smarter and smarter, and they got sucked into its center of gravity.

By one thirty there were seven teams involved, including the original proponents of the plan. That included the now three-man history-buff team and others who had taken casualties in battle, so the member total was thirty-six.

At that number, it was less of a squadron than a platoon—hence the name Operation Platoon.

With this much firepower at hand, surely they could beat even powerful foes with numbers alone, the participants gloated.

In accordance with the plan, they left the squad leaders behind, and twenty-nine armed soldiers headed for the mountain.

To wipe out M and his team.

CHAPTER 9

Ten-Minute Massacre I

SECT.9

CHAPTER 9
Ten-Minute Massacre I

At one thirty, M said, "Pito, you can still check out your device lying down. You should take a look. It's interesting."

She sat up from her nap, fallen leaves scattering from her cloak, then glanced at her Satellite Scan terminal. Her geometric brick-red facial tattoos stretched as she broke into a smile.

"Ah-ha-ha-ha. Very clever! Ah-ha-ha-ha-ha! So seven other teams are ganging up to form a coalition party, eh? Well, that's just lovely!"

She thrust her hands into the air gleefully, but it was clear from the body language of the masked men behind her that they were not pleased.

The short man spoke to M, but they all heard what he said. "What do you plan to do about this, M? If they all come after us at once, and without their squad leaders, it's going to be a major headache. Should we pull back?"

He seemed to be speaking for the other masked men, too. They waited for M to reply.

But it was Pitohui who responded, "So we'll just fight back and shoot 'em all dead, obviously!"

How? they all wondered but didn't ask aloud.

"M's going to tell us how," Pitohui said.

*   *   *

In the pub where the event was being aired, the impromptu conspiracy was the talk of the crowd. Some said it was a pathetic stunt; others said it was only against the unspoken rules, if not the written ones. Some even applauded it for being excellent strategy.

While the opinions were split all around, everyone in the room could agree with the one onlooker who commented, "Twenty-nine versus six, though… That's gonna be a great battle…"

PM4 was a powerhouse team with one of the two previous champions. They hadn't shot a single bullet yet in SJ2. How would they tackle a whole onslaught of enemies at once? The people were eager to find out.

They knew M was a mighty warrior. And it was clear that the four masked men had the eerie atmosphere of menacing talent.

That left just one question.

"I hope that princess doesn't trip them up…"

"Yeah, she's the one element of concern…"

"I mean, who wants to see a really fierce battle get broken up by some chick going 'Waaah, I'm so scared'?"

The camera followed the ascent of the twenty-nine up the mountain, starting at one thirty. It must have chosen this image for the tension it represented, as there was no other battle to cover during this time.

Because of this, the audience in the bar got to understand the lay of the mountain quite well. Its slope was steep, but it never became a cliff at any point. The ground was reasonably damp, enough to provide good grip. The twenty-nine warriors made quick progress.

However, there were boulders taller than a person jutting from the mountainside here and there that had to be avoided. The thick, tall trees also blocked their paths and sight lines. The farthest distance you could hope to see was less than fifty yards or so.

Streams rolled downhill here and there, burbling at the smaller points and rushing where the flow was thickest.

As you would expect from a patchwork alliance, the twenty-nine players wore a variety of garb.

At the very least, they did move in distinct teams. The seven groups each assumed formations around thirty-five feet in size, with the most agile character of each team serving as point and searching the area for signs of enemies. As they proceeded, they relayed the distance covered to the team leaders at the foot of the mountain, whom the cameras were also following.

They had drawn a map of the mountain in the dusty ground with sticks and pushed the markers for each team around with each update. Since they didn't have special map pieces, the markers were extra clips, grenades, and so on. It felt like a real command center that way.

The one-thirty scan had told them PM4's location. It was about a mile from the foot of the mountain. The twenty-nine soldiers headed for those coordinates. Perhaps the other squad would be gone by the time they reached the spot, but they might at least find some clues.

On the event stream, there was no sign of M's team. The audience had no idea where they were.

"They've gotta be aware of this conspiracy, though, right? And it'd obviously be the smart play to get out of the way, yeah?" said a man who was already several beers deep.

"But where would they run to? Down the north slope of the mountain, into the valley? They'll get caught eventually. And no matter what, their location's gonna pop on the forty-minute scan," replied a man who was several dozen jerky strips deep.

"So...you think they should fight back?"

"Against equal numbers, they'd have the advantage shooting down the slope. But with totals this lopsided..."

On the screen was a group of men climbing diligently. Each

one was carrying his very best gun, so they had quite a bit of fire-power. They had machine guns, and they had sniper rifles.

"…yeah, that's not gonna work…"

The man shook his head and gulped the last of his beer.

On the mountain, the men were in a state of excitement. The tough climb numbed their feet, but once they reminded them-selves that it was just a simulated sensation, it was easy enough to get past.

More importantly, their pace quickened with the thoughts of potential victory over a truly world-class opponent.

These men could see fellow squads nearby—players who had been potential foes just minutes ago. After they defeated the championship contenders, they'd turn on one another, of course, but that was its own problem. For now, they were teammates.

Light was weak on the mountain, and the rocks and trees impeded visibility, so there was no way to guess where shots might start coming from. But as soon as a single shot went off, PM4's location would be known—and they'd come under con-centrated fire from over twenty guns.

The men's advantage was so strong that it emboldened them to wish the other guys would shoot at them as they climbed. The more time passed with their advantage of numbers, the less con-cerned and cautious the men became.

In fact, after 1:37, they started saying things like, "I'm actually feeling sorry for those guys."

"Yeah, me too."

"Is whoever kills M going to get a special prize?"

"Should we start making bets? How about a pool on whether it's a grenade or a machine gun that does him in?"

They were feeling so confident that they started bantering among themselves on the ascent. Of course, those who were play-ing cautiously and trying not to give away their location found this chatter to be extremely annoying.

Finally, a man with a dark-red jacket snapped at a laughing member of a different squad nearby in beige desert camo. "Quiet! The plan said no talking aside from reports to base!"

While the scolded man's conversation partner clammed up after that, the one in desert camo himself clicked his tongue in distaste. "What the hell...? Who made you the leader of this group?"

He was itching for a fight. His comment also ruffled the feathers of the man in the red jacket.

"I'm not, you idiot—I'm just offering a sloppy jackass a bit of considerate education. You should thank me," he snapped back.

The two men stopped and glared at each other at a distance of ten yards. At the very least, they had enough presence of mind not to point their guns at each other.

"Once this is done...I'm gonna kill you."

"What a coincidence—I was just thinking the same thing. I won't forget your face and camo."

They were in agreement on something, at least.

Very shortly after that, the seven leaders back at the base sent the same instructions to all their squad members.

"Everyone, stop where you are. Prepare for the scan."

The men knelt in place, following the instructions.

"Half of you, keep an eye out. The other half, watch your screens."

It was forty seconds past 1:39, then fifty seconds...

"Scan will commence."

The fourth Satellite Scan of SJ2 began.

"Well, well. What's gonna happen now...?"

The scan results also displayed on the screen in the bar, so the audience there watched with bated breath just as the players did.

The scan started from the north, so the first piece of information was the continued survival of Team MMTM. Nobody was surprised by this.

Next, the scan showed LF at the western edge of the dome, SHINC on the southern side, and three squads inside it.

The promise of fierce battle at the dome was exciting, but the mountain region in the southeast was what everyone wanted to know about right now.

Where was PM4 now? Had they sensed the incoming enemy and descended the mountain to the north? Or had they moved farther to the east?

The scan showed…

"They're close! About five or six hundred feet northeast of the group!"

The seven team leaders issued surprised commands to their companions. PM4 was in a location on the slope very close to the platoon. Naturally, the players checking their Satellite Scan terminals on the mountain noticed this at the same moment and were understandably shocked.

They'd moved only a tiny bit north since the last scan. It seemed that PM4 had chosen to stay on the mountain and fight.

They couldn't see the enemy, due to poor visibility, but six hundred feet was close enough for battle. Bullets might come flying through the trees at any moment. Some of the soldiers even hoisted their guns just in case.

But the shots weren't coming.

"I guess they haven't spotted us yet…"

With as many people as they had moving as a group, there was no other obvious conclusion, so they related this to their squad leaders. The council of seven came to a quick decision. There was nothing to worry about anymore.

"Everyone, head to the location on the scan! Roll over them and wipe them out!"

The leaders placed one of their Satellite Scanners, which would have no more use for the next ten minutes, onto their dirt map to serve as the enemy's location marker.

"Everyone, head to the location on the scan! Roll over them and wipe them out!"

The faces of the twenty-nine soldiers broke into fierce smiles at this order. Now that they knew where the enemy was, there was just one thing to do: head for them. They picked up speed, everyone wanting the glory of being the first to strike.

The leaders gave them all detailed instructions on which way to head. The platoon covered about three hundred feet, fanning out around their destination point.

"Oh, what? Dammit...," the man closest to the target grunted. He reported, "Leader, we just ran into the biggest gorge yet. It looks about...a hundred feet across, going from east to west."

The men coming up from the rear came to a stop there, too. The river gouged the side of the mountain, spanning a hundred feet wide and thirty feet deep. Dotting the surface here and there were rocks about as tall as a person, the water rushing between them.

"Requesting orders. Is the destination upstream?"

The leader's response was immediate and affirmative.

"Then we can't reach the target without descending into the valley. So what now?"

This answer took a bit longer to arrive.

The seven squad leaders had to make a split-second decision. If they spent too long debating, they might lose their grasp on PM4's location. So they discussed the situation quickly and briefly before coming to their decision.

"Leave one team on the left side of the valley and one on the right, so they're worried about an attack from above. The rest of you, descend into the valley and keep going."

*   *   *

Teams of four and five spread out on either side of the valley, and the other twenty men began to walk through it. The man-size rocks were scattered all over, and many of them were damp or slick from the water, so walking along them was challenging.

Still, knowing that the enemy would be ahead kept them excited and motivated. And in fact, the rocks might even serve as cover against bullets. The men carefully made their way from rock to rock, mindful that enemy fire might come at any moment.

Once they were about two hundred or so feet from their destination, they saw something.

"What the heck is that?"

Others could see the same thing from a height well over the platoon's shoulders—the audience from the pub. The camera was located in the air over the valley, following their backs as they went.

"A waterfall…"

Up ahead, at the top of the far side of the valley, was a large waterfall about fifty feet tall, with a stream over fifteen feet across. The water rumbled and splashed ceaselessly, slamming the earth below.

Naturally, this was the end of the gorge. It had narrowed to about twenty yards across here and ended in this fifteen-yard cliff. The only players who could climb this were the ones with points in the Climbing skill. The rest would need a good rope setup.

One of the men on the scene reported, "It's a waterfall. Pretty big one. I live in a multigenerational four-floor building with a storefront on the ground, and it's about the same size."

"Way to break the atmosphere," someone else grumbled under his breath.

"Is this the right spot on the scan? You're sure it's this waterfall? Over."

The answer came back at once. The man shouted to his fellow companions so he could be heard over the deafening water. "He says that's where the scan indicated! Right at the falls!"

"Are they above 'em? Hey, can the teams that took the high ground see anything?" he asked. Through the relay of home base, he got his answer.

"They don't see anything! The only thing above the falls is the river that flows down it!"

It had now been three minutes since the last scan. Someone checked his watch and wondered, "Did they move already? Did they clear out on us?"

Another teammate replied, "Maybe... That was a swing and a miss, I guess."

Then a man from a different squad who was nearby shook his head. "Actually...I'm not so sure about that..."

"Why not?"

"How can you tell?"

The man answered, "I just noticed... You see how the top of that waterfall juts out?"

The top? The other two men leaned out from their rock cover and saw what he was talking about. The river flowed over the edge of the cliff, where a rocky outcropping extended from the wall, forming a water curtain that wasn't flush with the cliff side.

Meaning that if they followed the rocks to either side, they could actually get behind the waterfall.

"There's enough space back there for someone to hide..."

At last, the group of squad leaders understood what was happening.

Their prey was trying to hide behind the waterfall. If the platoon went past them without finding them, then they could rush down the mountain and escape to a different area of the map while the twenty-nine wandered around in search of life.

Well, that wouldn't be happening now. Their decision was firm and instantaneous.

The squad leaders issued orders.

"There's an extremely high chance the enemy is hiding behind the waterfall. All units open fire with maximum lethality."

The twenty soldiers located in the gorge raised their muzzles one after the other. Snipers and machine gunners propped their weapons up on the rocks with bipods. The submachine gunners and assault-rifle users hunched down next to hard stone for support.

They aimed for the curtain of water a few dozen yards ahead. The valley was narrow enough that they couldn't all fan out for better angles.

"If you're in front, don't you dare raise your head, or you'll catch a bullet in the back of the skull!" shouted a man with a machine gun resting on a rock. They set up like a formal group photo, with the people in front lower and the ones in the back aiming higher.

One guy who was ready to go asked, "Will our bullets actually shoot through the water?"

"Dunno. I guess we'll find out, yeah?"

"True."

Five team leaders issued simultaneous orders:

"Fire!"

Twenty guns opened fire at once in the narrow gorge.

There was a sound like an explosion, followed by a strange pattern on the curtain of falling water. Jets of water erupted sideways, dropping at the same speed as the waterfall itself as they extended outward and disappeared into the ground.

The bullets pierced through the water, though perhaps not all of them did. This was proved by the machine guns' tracer bullets, which bounced off of—presumably—the rocks behind the waterfall and deflected out the side of the falls.

"It'll work! Fire, fire, fire!"

"Yeah!"

They were merciless. If the six were indeed hiding behind the falls, they'd be massacred in mere moments.

Twenty guns roared and burst—the sound unabated. It echoed off the walls of the narrow canyon and lasted longer in the air before dying out, creating an unholy cacophony. If it weren't for *GGO*'s automatic volume adjustment, they all would've experienced hearing loss.

The firing continued.

Machine gunners replaced ammo belts. The others switched out their magazines for new ones, over and over. Empty cartridges in *GGO* vanished within a few seconds and produced little sparkles as they did so. The sight of dozens and dozens of cartridges flying through the air to land on rocks and water before sparkling out of existence was practically spellbinding.

The gunpowder exhaust of twenty guns slowly filled the air and hung there. The canyon was as hazy as if they'd built a campfire.

"Holy cow! This is awesome."

"Yeah. I've never seen this much full-throttle fire in *GGO* at once..."

The nine men on either side of the gorge forgot about their mission to keep an eye out and soaked in the world's loudest percussion performance from their balcony seats.

"I wish we were down there, too. Did we get the short straw?"

After fifty seconds of madness, the squad leaders commanded, "Cease fire! That should be enough!" The gunfire abated bit by bit as each group let up.

"Raaah!" One last man, with an M40A3 sniper rifle, didn't notice the command until one of his teammates smacked him on the head. "Wha—? Huh?"

"You're the only one still shooting."

"Oh, sorry. One last shot, then—it's the last one in my clip."

He pushed his retracted bolt back into place and shot one more time into the waterfall. The sound echoed over and over, until the only sound in the valley was the rushing of the falls. The water had been so noisy before, and yet it seemed so quiet now.

The waterfall didn't look any different.

"Okay... Does anyone nimble wanna go check behind the falls now?"

Four players on separate teams all nominated themselves for the job. They all played high-agility characters with submachine guns.

"Take it away, then! All you're looking for is the DEAD marker. If they're still alive, finish 'em off."

"All right, we got this!"

"Don't trip and fall into the stream... That'll do a lot of damage."

"No problem!"

"If there's trouble, hit the deck, and we'll provide backup fire."

"Got it. Thanks!" said the intrepid scouts.

Normally, they would be opposing forces, but the act of all firing at the same target had instilled a strange kind of solidarity in them. The individual squadrons had finally become a true platoon.

The four scouts split into pairs to climb up either side. The remaining twenty-five men watched and waited, guns trained on the waterfall.

"I got shot a bit," Pitohui heard M say.

She excitedly replied, "You gonna die?"

"Sadly, I'll be fine."

"Oh, darn. I was going to avenge you and everything."

"Forget about me already. The table's been set. Now do as you wish."

"Oh, you don't need to remind me. Just give the signal!"

The four men approached the waterfall, making use of their high agility to swiftly hop from rock to rock. When they were about ten yards away, the man leading on the right lifted his Mini Uzi, while the leader on the left had his own MP7A1 SMG at the ready.

"The four guys are approaching the falls from both sides... Doesn't seem like they see anything yet," a platoon member reported back to the squad leaders.

Five yards to go. The closest man was already drenched from the spraying water.

Four yards. He rested his finger on the trigger. He held up his free hand to the two men on the other side.

He curled his fingers in, one at a time: a countdown.

Four, three, two...

With one second to go, the men exploded.

Bright bluish balls of fire erupted on either side of the falls, obliterating the four scouts.

The men at lead point flew fifteen feet into the air and crashed against the walls of the gorge. The other two were buffeted off-balance by their companions, and they toppled into the pummeling falls. The two explosions happened in perfect synchronization.

"Plasma grenades! They're alive! Hostiles in the waterfall! Shoot, shoot, shoot!"

The roar in the canyon began anew.

As though on cue, something arose on the mountainside.

It was a group of masked men. There were three of them, waiting in three holes in separate locations and covered in camouflage ponchos with dirt and dead leaves carefully placed on top. They all stood simultaneously.

The three had been hiding just five yards from the north edge of the canyon—right behind the group of men who were supposed to be watching the mountain slope above the waterfall. The platoon members could easily have stepped on their hiding spots.

The trio popped up with guns in hand and began firing at the backs of their defenseless targets.

*   *   *

The short man had a shotgun. It was a pump-action gun called a UTS-15, capable of fourteen consecutive shots. It had a jutting, blocky look, like one of the futuristic optical guns, along with two magazine tubes—a very strange-looking shotgun, indeed.

He made good use of the quick pump action to fire three double-aught bucks at each target. The storm of buckshot riddled the bodies of the four men standing at the lip of the gorge and staring down at the waterfall.

The tall man used a machine gun, a 7.62 mm German MG 3.

It was a historical model that was the same as the Nazi German MG 42, just with a different caliber muzzle—except that this particular gun also had the latest sound suppressor attached. The circular tube extending from the muzzle was called a suppressor rather than a silencer because it didn't eliminate sound quite as effectively.

The man held the long and heavy MG 3 at his waist, with a side-mounted bipod in his left hand. While his companion was blasting the men in front of them, he leaped onto a tall rock with leg power alone, then opened automatic fire from the top.

The suppressed muzzle issued a very strange bark: *Jaaa-ka-ka-ka-ka-ka-kan!* The ammunition belt hanging from the left side of the gun shuffled upward as it sucked in more bullets and spat them out forward. The empties ejected downward, pinging off the rock and bouncing away.

As he fired, he waved the barrel back and forth. This caused the spray of bullets to pass over the top of the canyon and pummel the five men who stood watching from the far side. Bullet-wound effects glowed all over their bodies, and they tumbled in place.

The one man lucky enough to survive the immediate onslaught lifted his Galil assault rifle where he'd collapsed to the ground, and he shouted, "En—!"

But he couldn't even get the word *enemies* out of his mouth.

Another bullet penetrated his right arm, then burrowed into his head, killing him instantly.

Right behind two platoon members, the chubby masked man cycled his gun's bolt and ejected a large empty cartridge. The erstwhile sumo wrestler held a large sniper rifle, which he'd just used to shoot the target's arm and head.

The gun was about four feet long, with an independent pistol grip and a flared stock like a fishtail: the Savage 110 BA. A very rare and powerful weapon in *GGO*, it shot powerful .338 Lapua Magnum rounds.

Within the span of three seconds, the nine soldiers on the top of the canyon were dead.

None of the platoon members inside the canyon realized this had happened. Their own gunfire was so noisy that they never heard the sounds of their comrades' assassins gunning them down. And because they had split up by teams, none of them would have seen the HP bars in the top left corner of their vision dropping to zero.

The first to realize what had happened were the team leaders back at the base. Two of the leaders noticed their teammates getting wiped out, but they assumed it was some mistake at first. Only when they noticed the other also going pale did they figure it out.

"My team is dead!"

"Mine, too! Wiped out!"

Once the other team leaders realized that these were the two teams atop the sides of the canyon, the picture clicked into place for everyone. They gave orders to their squads down inside the gorge.

"Hostiles above you! They wiped out your backup! Watch out above! Did you catch that?"

But they didn't hear any response from their companions.

"Why?"

It was the audience at the bar that had the most complete picture of what happened.

There was another battle happening elsewhere at the time, so the bar was split into two groups. The players watching *this* battle unfolding erupted into excitement when they saw the plasma grenades explode at the sides of the waterfall.

"Ooh!"

"Here we go!"

Thanks to the multiple screens, they had a clear view of the masked men when they popped up out of the ground. The camera switched angles to film from right behind them.

When they pointed their guns at the unsuspecting men staring down into the canyon, someone in the crowd jokingly shouted, "Behind you, behind you!" right before the shooting started.

Shotgun, machine gun, and sniper rifle knocked down their targets with practiced ease, much to the theatrical pity of the audience.

"Oh, man."

"That's what happens when you don't pay attention…"

Their curiosity turned to the masked men who had so efficiently slaughtered nine victims.

"If they just start blasting down into the canyon, you think they could kill all the guys down there?"

As it turned out, they did not. Rather than peering over the edge, they simply squatted in place and stayed still.

"How come?" wondered someone in the audience, right as the feed switched perspective. It was trained on a woman's back.

"It's her!"

The navy-blue suit and ponytail made it clear. She couldn't be mistaken for anyone else.

This was the woman with M and the masked men. She was

slowly making her way up the canyon, sneaking up from behind on the men still shooting at the waterfall.

"Why?" said someone, speaking for the rest of the crowd. "Why isn't she holding a weapon?"

Going by the feed, her hands were empty, and there were no holsters, grenades, or knives on her gear belt. They could certainly be in her inventory, but at the moment, she was totally unarmed.

"Is she going to…negotiate? Like, 'Hey, guys, wanna team up with us instead?' or something?" someone else wondered.

"Then why would the masked guys take out the ones at the top of the canyon?" another man pointed out.

What in the hell was that woman going to do? Nobody knew the answer.

She snuck from rock to rock until she reached the group of men at last. They were still firing ceaselessly into the waterfall, so nobody noticed her presence—despite the fact that their enemy was standing right behind them.

It was such a surreal sight on the video that it was almost creepy.

The camera swung around so that it framed the man at the very rear of the group, who was madly firing a Russian RPD light machine gun propped against a rock, and less than twenty feet behind him was a woman with tattoos on her cheeks.

Her sharp-featured face broke into a smile as she said something that the audience could not hear.

"I'm going in. Don't send backup."

1:46 PM.

The clock readout in the upper left corner of the video screen clearly displayed the time.

It was at that moment when the audience saw what the woman was doing.

She snuck up directly behind the man shooting the RPD light machine gun, grabbed the back of his collar with her right hand, and pulled. She made it look simple, but it must have taken a tremendous strength stat. The large, solid man was yanked clean away from his gun, which stopped firing.

Then she switched her grip from his collar to the back of his head—and viciously rammed his face into the rock.

The damage started right from the first blow. Damage effects burst from his nose—little glowing red particles that resembled blood spraying out of him.

Two, three, four—she continued slamming his face into the rock until the twitching man's limbs finally fell limp. A DEAD tag floated over his body.

That smooth, practiced sequence of events left the audience in the bar silent for a moment.

Then someone yelled, "Holy shit, she just iced that guy with her bare hands!"

"You can do that...?"

"Well, you can die from a fall, so blows do cause damage...but who would ever bother?" the men wondered.

Meanwhile, the woman tossed the body aside and picked up the man's RPD. She hauled the heavy machine gun up against her shoulder as if it were a simple rifle.

Then she fired it. Directly into the backs of the men in the canyon.

She wasn't aiming at anyone in particular, just spraying bullets back and forth. And yet, oddly enough, they all seemed to find her targets, who were between ten and seventy feet away. Three unlucky soldiers got hit in vital areas and were knocked clean out of SJ2 without ever realizing what had happened to them.

Surprised to find themselves under fire from behind, those members of the platoon who were lucky enough not to get hit turned around, mouths open, as if to say *Hey, you idiot, don't shoot the guys on your own side!*

One of them gaped in comical, slack-jawed disbelief as she shot him to death. The rest of them darted behind rocks to avoid the hail of gunfire.

It took just three seconds for her to use up whatever ammo was left in the gun she'd stolen. She tossed it aside, trotted to a rock, and leaped into the air—toward a gaping man crouching behind it.

Her knee protectors caught him square in the face.

The man toppled into the water that flowed between the rocks. She kicked him hard with the heel of her boot and yanked his AKM away from him, then started shooting it at the other men. As she did so, she stomped hard on the neck of the toppled man with her right foot.

He flailed his arms and legs as best he could, struggling to pull his face above the water, but he soon joined the list of casualties as a victim of drowning, after she'd shot three of his comrades with his own gun.

"Enemy fire!"

"Shoot her!"

They started to shoot back at last, gouging the rock the woman hid behind with bullets. A figure promptly leaped out from behind the rock, drawing all the gunfire to it.

The character took dozens of bullets to the body but did not die on account of them—it was already dead.

Like a snake, the woman slithered from rock to rock in the opposite direction of the corpse she'd thrown as a diversion. She emerged right beside a man who was desperately reloading his Remington Versa Max Tactical semiautomatic shotgun.

"Hiii!"

"Huh?"

He looked up right as she smashed him in the face with the stock of the empty AKM. It was a precise, uncompromising blow.

She dropped the AKM, snatched the Versa Max from the reeling man's hands, spun it downward, and blasted her off-balance prey in the face. His head lit up so bright from the damage effects that there was nothing visible above his nose. Dead, of course.

The woman then stuck her thumb into the loading chamber of the Versa Max. This helped her get an intuitive sense of how many shells were still in the ammunition tube. She was satisfied with what she felt, so she jumped ahead with her new weapon in hand.

Only eight survivors were left—there were more dead in the gorge than living now. There was no longer any organized resistance, just individuals hiding and making do on their own.

The woman gleefully made her way through the area. She didn't have the high agility of Llenn, but she was still as stealthy and nimble as a ninja.

She found a man hiding behind a rock, smiled, and pressed the large mouth of the shotgun to his neck before firing. The first shot only half severed his neck, so she pulled the trigger again to finish the job. Then she grabbed his head by the hair and tossed it into the air.

The camera switched angles, capturing the moment when the severed head dropped directly in front of another man hiding behind a rock.

The mic didn't pick up his scream, but the way he leaped up in terror was both visible and palpable. He scrambled around the rocks, trying to escape, splashing through the shallow river. Then he peered around one of the rocks, only to see the foot of the woman chasing him.

She blasted the back of his head with her shotgun, adding another one to the list of dead. Then she spotted three plasma grenades on the new body's waist and helped herself to them, immediately tossing two of the three.

They soared toward the waterfall, ten yards away—right to where two of the men who'd been knocked backward by M's grenades were finally pulling themselves free of the water. The projectiles plopped into the liquid one after the other, then produced two huge plumes of bulging water.

Water and body parts soared into the air, immediately replaced by the rushing of the falls—and two fresh bodies.

*   *   *

The men waiting at the top of the canyon cliffs didn't fire a shot.

Because of their vantage points, they could perfectly see all the enemies who were crouching and hiding behind the rocks. If needed, they could have easily shot anyone in position to harm their teammate.

But that moment never arrived.

"..."

They merely watched in silence as Pitohui gleefully darted around the canyon, performing her one-woman massacre.

On the screens, the audience saw four men hiding behind four rocks for dear life—as well as the woman searching for them.

She was on the opposite side of the stream, pulling a Beretta 92FS 9 mm semiautomatic pistol off a body, then continuing on her way. They were playing hide-and-seek, and she was it.

Around this point, the attitude of the audience switched on a dime. At first, they'd been horrified by her efficient, demonic slaughter.

"Get 'em! Only four left!"

"Don't shoot 'em, you guys on the cliffs! You've gotta respect the craft!"

"She's gonna get the max kills award, that's for sure!"

"Damn, lady, you are crazy!"

"Sorry for insinuating you were a geek-club princess!"

"I'd let you kill me!"

But now their opinions of her had done a total one-eighty.

"What's going on? What happened?"

The home base with all the team leaders was in a terrified panic.

First, they got no responses, then they heard screams and saw their squadmates' HP bars dropping until they were dead. Each team leader had so many casualties to report that it was impossible to keep up with them.

"There's someone real crazy out—"

Pshum!

It was easy to tell how close the shooter was by the way the victim's mic picked up the sound of the gunshot. The leader didn't even need to look at the HP bar to know what had happened.

The man covered in body protectors who had devised the plan in the first place confirmed that his own team was totally wiped out. "Is there...anyone...still alive...?"

Four of his fellow leaders shook their heads. Only two didn't.

"I've got one...but his hit points are in the yellow."

"Same thing, but red."

Their replies were somber.

"I think it's safe to come out now, M," said the chubby masked man. M emerged from behind the falls, his M14 EBR in hand.

He was utterly soaked, of course, and he featured six glowing damage points on his thick rear end and legs. He'd lost about 40 percent of his hit points.

The machine gunner at the top of the canyon noted, "They got you pretty good. Was there a hole in your shield?"

"Deflections. They hit the rock above me, and it ricocheted down at me. But I kept my spine and head covered."

"I told you it was dangerous. That was really reckless."

"I had to set the table, or it wouldn't have worked. Where's Pito?" M asked. He looked down the gorge, but all he could see were twenty glowing DEAD signs hanging in the air. It was practically unheard of to have that many clustered in such a tight space.

"She's further downstream. Around a big rock. Playing with the last two."

"...?"

M frowned with suspicion and leaped from rock to rock down the stream with surprising grace for someone so large. About twenty yards downstream, he found Pitohui. She was leaning against a huge boulder, a plundered Beretta 92FS in her hand.

"Oh dear."

She was watching two foes about five yards ahead of her.

One was a man in desert camo. His body was almost entirely submerged in the water, and he no longer had any feet. The glow from the damage effect was visible through the clear water.

The other was a man with a dark-red jacket. He had his left hand around a low rock in the fast-moving water, with his other hand trailing behind him. It was holding on to the collar of the desert-camo man's bulletproof vest. If he let go, the other man would wash away in the river.

"It's just those two left," M reported to Pitohui. "What are you waiting for?"

Pitohui turned back to him with a delighted smile. "See the guy holding the other one? He's still got a pistol at his side."

M looked. Indeed, the man in the burnt-red jacket had an old-fashioned leather holster with a .45-caliber Colt 1911A1 semiautomatic pistol inside: a "Government Model."

"I'm waiting for him to drop the dead weight, pull that out, and shoot me. I mean, it's just psychologically damaging to shoot an unresisting person, you know?" said Pitohui, giving herself far too much credit.

"Is that supposed to be a joke?" M asked honestly. "We don't have time to waste."

"Fine, fine."

She lifted the Beretta 92FS and fired it lazily. The bullet sank into the side of the jacketed man.

"Gah!"

His body jolted with the impact, but he didn't let go.

"Hmm? Persistent, aren'tcha?"

Pitohui shot him again. This one hit his right upper arm. It must've numbed the muscles terribly, but he still didn't let go.

"Hey, what's with all the hard effort?" Pitohui asked indignantly.

"Shut up!" the man in the jacket screamed. "Do you find it fun to torment an opponent who can't fight back? Do you?"

Pitohui didn't miss a beat. "Do you find it fun to torment six players with thirty?"

"…"

"Yes! The answer is 'Both are fun'! You know that, don't you? If you were in my place, you'd be doing the same thing!"

"…"

The man said nothing now. Instead, the other man, in the desert camo, who avoided being swept away only because his fellow victim had a grip on him, shouted, "Hey, enough! Let go! She's right! Pull out your Government and shoot her! Blast her brains out!"

"…I refuse."

"You moron!"

"I might despise your rotten guts, but we're still on the same side until we beat them. And on my team, we don't abandon our comrades."

"…If you die, it's basically the same thing!"

"But we're not done yet! I'm confident that our team leaders listening in will do something about it!"

"…Yeah, I guess you're right!"

The two men were getting very worked up on their own, without her input.

"Hey, don't ignore me," Pitohui said, firing twice. Both shots hit the chest of the man submerged in the water, but a DEAD tag didn't light up.

"Oh, is that armor? Or did the water dull the velocity? This is what I hate about pistols. And I'm out of ammo, too."

The slide of the Beretta 92FS in her hand locked back into place, the signal that it was empty. Pitohui tossed the paperweight into the water.

"M, let me see your EBR."

"No. I don't have ammo to waste on games."

"Tch. Fine, I'll take something off a body. Now, which one do I want…?"

Pitohui left the side of the rock and began to search the area for a new weapon.

From the rock where he stood, M told the two men, "You warn your leaders. Tell them to surrender."

"..." "..."

The men didn't reply, so M calmly continued, "It wasn't a bad plan you had. You did well. But this is how it turned out. The seven survivors banding together still don't stand a chance."

Pitohui returned, looking serious. "Hey, stop that! That's no fun! You two, forget what this musclehead just said and tell your leaders, 'They tortured us! We're humiliated! Please, sirs, avenge our defeat!' Got that?!"

"Yeah, they'll come back and slaughter you all!" shouted the man in the dark jacket.

"You're all going down!" said the man in desert camo with a grin.

"Yes, yes, that's more like it," Pitohui said, satisfied. She gave a plasma grenade she'd scavenged an underhand toss.

"Dammit!"

"Go to hell, bitch!"

The grenade exploded in the river a moment later, turning the shouting men into a dozen separate pieces.

A right hand still firmly held a collar.

"Yeaaaaaah!"

"Awesome! She really took out eighteen guys on her own!"

The bar was in a commotion.

"No wonder they're championship contenders!"

"What a hell of a show! Bravo!"

But as earsplitting as the cheering was, none of it reached the mountain canyon.

"Shall we move on to the next one, then? Let's meet up downstream, boys," Pitohui said, walking away.

"Wait—I have to go get my shield," M warned. He hurried back up the stream for his trusty screen, which was still deployed behind the waterfall.

"Make it quick."

Pitohui then looked up at the four masked men who were staring down at her. The river carried the scattered body parts of the last two victims downstream.

Unlike the BoB, Squad Jam didn't leave bodies in their grotesque, mutilated state, so they would reform into human shape further on—but for now, it was a horrific sight.

Despite the fact that their masks covered their faces, Pitohui seemed to understand what they wanted to say.

"They're not going to be good friends without an experience like that," she insisted with a smile. "Just watch, ten minutes from now they'll be sharing drinks back at the bar!"

How much of what she says and does is actually honest? the men wondered, but no one would speak this question aloud.

"What...the hell...? Dammit!"

In a field at the foot of the mountain a mile away, the man dressed all in plastic protectors who had come up with the whole idea spat and swore.

The status readout made it clear: His teammates were all dead. Only he, the team leader, was still alive. And it was the same for the other six leaders, too. They had no eyes on what unfolded, so they didn't even know how their companions had died.

"They're definitely all gone..."

"Yeah...I can't believe it..."

They all wore the same pained expression. One of them, the man dressed like an Imperial Japanese officer, said, "I'll be going, then," and marched off—his Type 100 submachine gun in hand—toward the looming mountain.

"What are you going to do?" asked the man in the protectors.

The officer turned back and said, "Sadly, this operation was a failure. So now I will be carrying out my own fight."

"Uh...that sounds very cool and all, but I don't understand what action that corresponds to."

"Oh, pardon me. I am going to fight the demons who live on that mountain until I perish. I am sure that I will not survive, but resigning now would only shame myself before my companions."

"..."

"The plan itself wasn't a bad one. We all joined it of our own volition. This wasn't your fault. It was a short alliance, but an enjoyable experiment we engaged in together. I pray for your success in battle."

He finished with a beauty of a salute, then turned on his heel.

As he marched away, his silhouette growing smaller, the remaining six leaders started walking without a word.

"What? What's the meaning of this?" the Imperial Japanese officer wondered when the other six caught up to him.

"Should be obvious. We're fighting with you. We might be on different teams, but our goal is the same. You play *Gun Gale*—you should get it."

"Yeah, exactly! We're not gonna let you hog all the cool lines!"

"They've got six. We've got seven. Piece of cake!"

"If we each kill one, someone's gonna be the rotten egg. So you'd better be quick about it."

"I'll avenge my team. I haven't had a chance to shoot once yet, so this is perfect for me."

"Let's be clear: Our SJ2 starts right now."

Once they'd all said their fill, the Imperial Japanese officer broke into a smile.

"Then let's stand and fight together—brothers."

The camera caught sight of seven warriors marching in a line to the mountain of evil in the distance.

Their clothes and weapons were all over the place. The only thing they shared in common was slaughtered teammates.

The audience in the bar was split on how to feel about this.

"Wait, you guys are gonna go fight them after all that?! They'll wipe you out! Just resign now, and you won't have to suffer the misery of defeat."

"They can't win... They just can't."

"I don't mind, if it means I get to see that lady kick ass some more."

Those people were all certain of PM4's victory.

"Damn, those dudes are real men! Hell yeah!"

"I think I'm getting teary-eyed... It's just like that movie, the Seven Whatchamacallits."

"You got this, guys! You've still got a chance!" cheered their supporters in the crowd.

But there was one thing the entire audience shared in common: a feeling that said *Aw yeah, we're gonna get another kickass battle out of this.*

On the screens in the bar, the seven warriors strode toward the distant mountain, backs to the camera.

In just a few hundred yards, the farmland ended, and the treacherous, rocky slope began.

What kind of furious fight would they put up? The crowd in the bar watched with intense interest—as the line of seven instantly turned into six.

He didn't run.

The man on the right end suddenly split down the middle. His top half slid backward, and his bottom half toppled forward.

"Huh?"

Two seconds later, they were five.

In a similar fashion, the man on the left end split into two pieces.

The feed switched angles. Now it showed that woman with the ponytail and facial tattoos again, standing in the woods, aiming an enormous rifle. Her gun was propped up on a flat rock with a bipod stand, while around her sat M's shield, which had been deployed to such memorable effect in the last Squad Jam.

"Ooh! An M107A1 antimateriel rifle!" someone in the audience shouted.

Nobody needed to ask what that was. Unless you were brand-new to the game, pretty much any gun fanatic playing *GGO* had taken a crash course in that weapon already.

The M107A1 was a 12.7 mm antimateriel rifle manufactured by Barrett Firearms in America. It was an improved version of the well-known M82—it was lighter and had a muzzle designed for use with a sound suppressor.

There was one attached to the M107A1 on the screen, in fact. That added another sixteen inches to a rifle that was already five feet long. The woman wasn't short by any means, but this weapon was practically a spear, the way it rivaled her own height.

An antimateriel rifle using bullets that size could shoot accurately over 1,600 yards—and even farther than that if the conditions were good, such as at high altitudes with thin air.

As they watched, she fired a third time.

Even dampened, the noise was considerable, and gas blasted from the apertures on either side of the suppressor muzzle. It was an automatic, so an empty cartridge that was an astonishing four inches long emerged from the right side of the gun.

The giant bullet roared through the air at the distant men, who were still a good 1,300 yards away.

After a journey that lasted two seconds, the bullet hit home in the third target—the man in the protectors, who wasn't aware of why two of his companions had collapsed yet.

But thanks to his sci-fi armor, the human-cleaving power of the 12.7 mm round did not kill him. The chest protector he wore passed the limit of what it could resist and shattered like ceramic—and his weighted body flew ten feet backward, but he lost only about 40 percent of his hit points.

"Urgh... Dammit..."

And in the very next moment, he lifted his torso into the path of the second bullet, which was hit in exactly the same spot as the first.

Stuck in the middle of an open field with no cover or escape, the remaining four flattened themselves on the ground.

"Enemy's dead ahead! Don't drop your line of sight! Watch for the bullet line! Get ready to dodge!" said one of them, listing the practical steps for avoiding a sniper in *GGO*.

But the Imperial Japanese officer got up and ran. "We can't! They shoot without a bullet line! Just get up and run! Make your way into the trees as quick as you can!"

He made a beeline for the woods. There was no place to hide, and no other way to survive than to get to the cover of the trees.

The other three watched him go. They didn't chase after him. If you hadn't experienced a battle against a lineless sniper, it wouldn't click for you. You wouldn't feel the fear it inspired.

"We know where they are... As long as we watch for the line, they can't snipe us..."

At that exact moment, one of those very bullet lines appeared from halfway up the mountain. Given the distance involved, it arced upward quite a bit and descended down toward them, curving a bit left.

When the line slid sideways and crossed one of the men's bodies, he moved to his right. "Ha!"

He rolled until he was a good ten feet away from the line before stopping.

"How was that?" he said proudly, right before a bullet *without* a line hit him in the face, killing him instantly.

"That was cool. Let's do it again—the guy on the left. And shoot this time," Pitohui commanded the chubby man, who was set up with his sniper rifle about twenty yards to the side of her.

"Yes'm," he said, squatting behind the tripod-mounted Savage 110 BA. The man peered through the scope, aiming in the general direction of the prone target. While this gun didn't have the power of the 12.7 mm, it could also effectively shoot 1,600 yards.

The chubby man brushed the trigger, placing the bullet circle that appeared in the scope over the man lying in the field. That produced a bullet line, too, of course, so the man moved quickly and laterally to avoid it.

The Savage 110 BA fired, its bullet flying faster than the speed of sound, until it sent up a cloud of dust a ways away from the man. The dust dissipated almost as soon as it appeared, right in place.

"Got 'em."

Pitohui fired the M107A1.

Like M had before, she shot without using a bullet circle. Through personal experience and calculation, she accounted for the pull of gravity over its long interval, the effect of wind, and even the slight curve of Earth's rotation.

The range was exactly the same as her last shot. The dust her teammate's shot had kicked up had told her there was no wind to worry about.

The 1.5-ounce bullet slowed from air resistance, but it still reached a speed of 390 mph before hitting the man in the back. It obliterated his torso and killed him immediately. That left one man still in the field.

"Okay, here we go," Pitohui murmured to herself, zeroing in on him with the scope. Then she saw that he was flat on his back, waving his left hand around in the air.

"No! Don't do it, you idiot!" she pleaded, but to no avail. Before she could fire, he completed the action and resigned. The lifeless left hand fell to the ground.

"Damn. I wanted to kill him…"

"One of them's coming this way. Below and to the left. Eleven hundred yards and approaching," M reported, reading the measurements on his large binoculars.

"Ooh." Pitohui turned the M107A1 toward him, but there were thick trees blocking her shot now. "Aw, damn. Can't get him. Shit! I wanted to shoot 'em all myself. Oh well. You guys can handle him."

She flipped the safety on the M107A1 and tenderly caressed its blocky body, which looked like it was lined with thin metal plates. "Nice job, baby. You're such a good girl. I wish I could take you back to Japan with me."

Less than a minute later, the MG 3 found its target and fired silenced shots that sprayed dirt around the vicinity of the Imperial Japanese officer.

The man kept going, desperately sidestepping and strafing to avoid the many bullet lines bearing down on him—until M's M14 EBR caught him with a trio of shots, and he toppled over about six hundred yards from the forest.

The final member of the platoon perished at 1:49 PM.

It was a ten-minute massacre.

Back in the bar, the topic of conversation was not the miserable end of the magnificent seven, but the antimateriel rifle the woman was shooting.

"There's still only one Barrett M107A1 on the Japanese server, right?"

"There better not be a bunch of them lying around."

"There are only nine confirmed antimateriel rifles and two rumored ones. They're all different makes, naturally. But some people think that since we've found newer ones, there might be more out there."

"That chick Sinon who kicked ass at the last BoB used one, too, right? What was it? The British AW50?"

"Close, but wrong. It's the Hecate II from France. Wooden stock model."

"Oh, that one."

"You really know your stuff. You her groupie or something?"

"Hell no! I got matched against Sinon in the BoB prelims. She blew my head off with that thing from nine hundred yards away!"

"Rest in peace, good buddy... That musta been real hard on you..."

"Don't console me. That just makes it worse."

One man said, "Actually, guys, I know a bit about the owner of that M107A1. I heard some rumors from a while back..."

The others stopped talking so they could listen in.

"The guy beat a real tough quest and was lucky enough to win it as loot, but it was so rare and valuable, he could never take it out with him. Can you imagine if you had such a legendary gun, and you lost it in a random drop when you got killed? I'd die of shock."

"So...you think it was one of the masked guys? Like the BoB, you don't lose your weapon in Squad Jam, and in a team battle, you might actually make good use of an extreme outlier weapon like an antimateriel. Just like in this situation."

"Could be true. Or maybe the guy was afraid to use it or didn't have the ability or stats, so he just up and sold it to some fat-cat player. I have no idea what the truth is."

"I guess the skinny guy who hasn't shot once is the team's mule. He had it stored in his inventory."

"And that chick just sniped 'em dead from that distance? How many skills does she have up her sleeve?!"

"Speaking of the Barrett's owner," said a man acting like he knew what was up. If he'd had glasses, it would've been the kind of moment when he'd push them upward in a cool, knowing way. But he didn't wear any. "This clears up one thing."

Then he paused, milking the moment.

"...What's that?" someone said, realizing that he wasn't going to continue unless he was specifically asked.

"That team is obviously going to win this thing by a mile, right? You've got M with his shield, and the masked guys have tremendous skills of their own, with powerful weapons to boot. And to top it all off, there's that demon woman. No way any other team is going to come in and beat them."

The men around him all nodded sagely at this assessment.

"Hey! You guys!" shouted a man from another group, who'd been watching a different screen over the last ten minutes. "Why didn't you watch Llenn fight?! She's incredible! If she keeps going like this, she's gonna win this thing by a mile!"

To be continued...

AFTERWORD

Hello, everyone, I am your author, Keiichi Sigsawa.

Thank you very much for picking up this book, titled *Sword Art Online Alternative Gun Gale Online, Vol. 2: Second Squad Jam: Start.*

Once again, I will treat this afterword segment seriously.

Listen, maybe it's time I stopped writing so much weird nonsense in my afterwords that makes readers worry about me, or maybe I should quit writing stuff on the inside of my covers that wreaks havoc on the libraries that put protectors over their books. Maybe it's time to graduate from these shenanigans...

I mean, I'm going to be forty-three this year (2015), so maybe it's time to settle down. Most people would normally have a kid in high school by this point. And yet, I'm still single—owing to my lack of opportunity with women—but it's still late enough in life that I feel I shouldn't be jumping up and down and pounding my keyboard, shouting, "Yahoo! Afterword! I'm gonna whip up something nobody's ever seen before back here!"

It's time for a mature, grown-up afterword. A ripened afterword. I'm not really sure what that is, but you get the gist of it.

My point is, this afterword is very normal.

As always, there will be no spoilers in here. That's the one whatchama-thingy I will never break.

*   *   *

So...

Gun Gale Online, this spin-off set in the world of *Sword Art Online*, has now stretched into multiple volumes.

This is all thanks to those of you who bought the first volume!

It did have "1" in the name, so clearly I was thinking in terms of a multipart series, but that was not the same as actually having that come to pass. To put it in very stark terms, if I hadn't sold a single copy of the first volume, this book would not exist. So I am extremely grateful that we are here.

This volume revolves around the second Squad Jam event, and little pink Llenn is front and center again! Other characters from the first book appear, too, of course! To say any more would be a spoiler, so if you're reading this first, do enjoy the book!

Also, like the first volume, the majority of this book depicts a bunch of virtual gunfighting. There's no tender romance between star-crossed lovers, no space opera about a war for the fate of the galaxy, no controversial nihilistic depictions of youths with no outlet for their rage. Please read with confidence.

Also, Volume 2 is labeled *Start*, meaning the later Volume 3 will be the concluding *Finish* of this arc. That's right—the story continues.

I should've been able to wrap it up in one, but partway through, I realized what an incredible number of pages I'd already written. The fact that I had to change plans on the fly and stretch the story to an extra book is something only my editor and I know, so I won't mention it here. In fact, it was always planned that we'd go to three books. Why would it ever be anything different?

What's the final scenery Llenn will see in the world of guns and gales?

Who will win the second Squad Jam?

Who's the new blond girl on the cover of this volume? What will she do?

What's the mystery behind Pitohui and M?

Will Sigsawa actually buy more air guns and pretend they're for research?

All these mysteries and more will be revealed in Volume 3.

It's slated to come out on June 10th (in Japan). Hope you look forward to it.

I'll get back to my acknowledgments now. First of all, my heartfelt thanks to Reki Kawahara for allowing me to use the wonderful world of *Sword Art Online* to my own ends. The game system of *Gun Gale Online* is so brilliantly put together; I could tell as I was writing that, knowing my own meager experience playing video games, I would never have come up with such an idea.

If virtual reality games ever become a thing like this, I'm terrified I'll get so addicted that I'll forget to write, and I'll blow past all my deadlines. It's pure terror.

My editor's avatar approaches, ready to strike.

"Write your damn manuscriiiipt!"

"Never! Yaaaaaah!"

Bullets and ideas shoot back and forth. A ferocious battle ensues.

It's all very easy to imagine…but fortunately, there are no such games at the moment in 2015, so I'm betting Volume 3 will come out safe and sound.

Until we meet again in the next afterword.

Keiichi Sigsawa—March 10th, 2015

SPECIAL TEARJERKER EPIC
I Fight with My Pride on the Line!
~Let the Gunshot of My Soul Ring
Across the Dunes~

"Dammit! I'm the freakin' sponsor!"

A man screamed, but the camera did not pick up his voice.

Thirteen minutes after the start of the first Squad Jam, a character was shouting alone in the desert zone. He had an unremarkable avatar and wore unremarkable battle gear. The only remarkable thing he had was his gun, an automatic 5.56 mm sniper rifle, the SIG SG 550 Sniper.

It was a sniper-rifle version of the SG 550, a precision assault rifle used in the Swiss Army. The grip and stock were redesigned for sniping, and a much tougher and thicker barrel increased its accuracy. It had a scope, too, of course.

This was a very expensive gun in real life, and it was quite rare to find one in *GGO*. If you wanted to get one at an in-game auction, you'd be looking at a hefty sum.

The man was flat on his stomach in the desert, alone. A number of other men, presumably his teammates, were also lying on the dunes, but they all had DEAD signs floating over their backs.

"I'm the sponsor! How could this happen?! Dammit!" he fumed, but still, the camera didn't pick up his voice.

Then he got a message from somebody. A number of brilliant red lines started glowing around his vicinity, coming from the distance. The message was *There will be bullets flying here soon.*

"Eep!"

Despite all his rage, he still had enough presence of mind to notice them.

"Hyaaa!"

He wailed piteously and got to his feet, holding up the precious SG 550 Sniper. An instant later, bullets came flying along the paths of the lines.

There was the sound of air screaming as they zipped past, the dull buffeting of the sand where they struck, and the distant drumming of the gunfire itself, hundreds of yards in the distance.

"But I'm the sponsorrrr! I'm scared, I'm scared, I'm sca— Aiiee! Please, stop!" he blubbered, clutching his gun to his chest as he ran. It was open desert, so if they were shooting, that meant they'd moved until he was within range. He'd have to run to safety now.

But machine guns weren't that accurate, so if he ran as fast as he could, it was unlikely they'd hit him. He also knew where they were shooting from now, so once he found a place to hide and calm down, he could shoot back with his excellent sniper rifle.

"Just you wait. You'll taste the wrath of the sponsor's counterattack! Oh yes, you will soon understand the difference in accuracy between a machine gun and a sniper rifle, oh yes…," he gloated with a creepy smile.

The enemy had stopped firing for now, so he threw himself to the sand behind a dune.

Then he turned the SG 550 Sniper in the direction that he'd seen the muzzle flashes in the distance, and he peered through the scope.

"Heh! My brilliant, lethal sniping will send you to eternal rest... But I'll give you time to pray first... As you pass, you will etch into your heart the name of the man who was your Angel of Death... My name is—"

In the midst of this extremely embarrassing speech—the kind that would promptly make even his own parents pretend to be unrelated to him—he released the safety and put his finger to the trigger.

"—*Bohwuk!*"

A bullet-wound effect burst from his head, and he jerked once and then toppled over, lifeless. He'd never actually said his name. A DEAD tag appeared over his body.

About a thousand feet away, a pretty woman with black hair set down the Dragunov rifle she'd fired just once.

"You know, he seemed to be muttering something with a smile. What would it be? Do Japanese chant some kind of curse before they snipe?" she asked the dwarfish woman next to her, who'd been providing covering fire with a PKM machine gun.

"Dunno. I've never heard of such a thing," the other woman admitted, shrugging.

It was the end of one more character in the chaos of Squad Jam.

The End

Hello! This is
Kouhaku Kuroboshi.

When I was searching
for reference photos
of military gear
online, I found a
picture of a soldier
resting his arms inside
a plate carrier like this.
It seemed rather
charming to me.

How cute.

KURO

▼ Manga ▼ Light Novels

©REKI KAWAHARA/
NAOKI KOSHIMIZU

©REKI KAWAHARA
ILLUSTRATION: SHIMEJI

▶▶▶ ACCEL · WORLD

Art: Hiroyuki Aigamo
Original Story: Reki Kawahara
Character Design: HIMA

©REKI KAWAHARA/HIROYUKI AIGAMO

▼ ACCEL WORLD Manga

▼ ACCEL WORLD Light Novels

©REKI KAWAHARA   ILLUSTRATION:HIMA

©KEIICHI SIGSAWA
©REKI KAWAHARA
©TADADI TAMORI

©REKI KAWAHARA   ILLUSTRATION: KOUHAKU KUROBOSHI

◀ Kawahara's
newest series:

*SWORD ART ONLINE ALTERNATIVE
GUN GALE ONLINE*
MANGA AND LIGHT NOVELS